Marking Time

Sherryl D. Hancock

VULPINE
PRESS

Originally self-published by Sherryl D. Hancock in 2017

Published by Vulpine Press in the United Kingdom in 2017

ISBN 978-1-910780-40-4

Cover by Armend Meha

Cover photo credit: Tirzah D. Hancock

www.vulpine-press.com

Acknowledgements

Thank you to all law enforcement in all areas for all that you do and for laying your lives on the line to protect us all. With the utmost respect and appreciation, thank you!

To the love of my life, Tirzah, who's made it possible to share these books with all of you. It was Tirzah's refusal to give up on getting my books published that got these books out there. Thank you, my love!

Chapter 1

"Come on in," Catalina Roché said to the young woman standing at her office door.

Raine Mason did her best to tamp down on her nervousness. She'd heard that the Special Agent Supervisor wanted to talk to her, and she wondered if they were sending her back to the Sheriff's Office. She'd observed the new SAS all morning. Catalina Roché was not what Raine had been expecting. She was far from tough looking like the last SAS had been; the man had been a tank with legs. Catalina was about an inch shorter than Raine at five foot seven, and she had long, straight honey-blond hair. She was very feminine looking, but the nasty looking gun she wore on her hip next to her badge, hardened her a bit.

Raine had heard music coming from the office all morning, and one of the guys on the team had grinned and told her to get used to it. Raine didn't mind at all, in fact a lot of the music she'd heard she really liked; it was rhythmic, much like the music Raine herself listened to all the time. She'd also seen another woman in Catalina's office, and they had been talking and moving things around. She'd heard a lot of laughing going on, and assumed that this woman was a friend of Catalina's and not another employee.

Looking at this other woman now, Raine saw that she had long, dark wavy hair with gold colored eyes which seemed to glow against her tanned skin.

"You wanted to see me, ma'am?" Raine asked, her eyes on Cat who was seated behind the desk.

"Yes," Cat said, smiling over at the other woman. "Deputy Mason, this is Jovina Azevedo, my girlfriend."

"Nice to meet you, ma'am," Raine said, her tone formal.

"Oh my, it's nice to meet you too," Jovina responded, looking over at Cat widening her eyes slightly. "I'm gonna go, babe," she said, moving to stand and then leaning in to kiss Catalina.

"Okay, see you later," Cat said, smiling at Jovina.

Jovina left and Cat looked back at Raine, her sky-blue eyes bright. "Relax, Deputy, this isn't an inquisition," she said with a grin. "And have a seat, you're making my neck hurt."

Raine sat down, still nervous despite Cat's assurances.

Cat sat back in her chair, her eyes on Raine, assessing her. The girl had dark auburn hair that was pulled back into a bun at the nape of her neck, and the lightest blue eyes Cat had ever seen. She was very conservative looking; the only indication of any kind of wild side was the multiple earrings in either ear. Cat thought there was likely at least five in each ear. None of the earrings she wore particularly stood out, but the fact that she had them didn't jive with the rest of her appearance, so it was notable.

"I've read your file," she told Raine, "but why don't you tell me a little about yourself."

"About myself?" Raine asked. "In terms of what, ma'am?"

"Call me Cat," Catalina said, "and in terms of how you came to be here, how you got into law enforcement, maybe why you got into it. That kind of thing."

Raine nodded, uncertain.

"I grew up in Spanish Harlem in New York. I used to be a dancer, but then I came to California and decided to go into law enforcement, so I applied, got into the academy and started working for the Sheriff's Office. I got the chance to join this task force and grabbed it," Raine rattled it off so quickly Cat had to pause long enough to assimilate all the girl had said.

Shaking her head, Cat said, "From dancer to cop, that doesn't equate."

Raine shrugged. "Dancers don't make much money, you definitely can't live on it in California."

"Okay," Cat said, feeling like there was more to that story than she was hearing, but willing to let it go, for now. "Now, tell me about your time here."

"I started with LA IMPACT a year ago. Six months into my time here, there was an explosion at a meth lab and I got hurt. I've been out since then." Again, Raine ran through the explanation so quickly Cat struggled to keep up.

Cat narrowed her eyes at the young woman sitting across from her. "Is that a New York thing?"

"What, ma'am?" Raine asked.

"Talking a mile a minute," Cat said.

Raine pressed her lips together, looking contrite. "I guess so," she said, trying to make a point of talking slower.

Cat nodded, but she also noticed that Raine's foot was bouncing constantly.

"Are you nervous?" Cat asked.

"Yes ma'am."

"What are you afraid of?" Cat asked.

"That you're going to send me back to the SO," Raine replied, her speech quickening again.

"I'm not," Cat said simply.

Raine looked back at her for a long moment, blinking a couple of times. Then she visibly relaxed as she nodded.

"What I do want to talk to you about, though," Cat said, "is whether or not you might be coming back too soon."

"I'm not, ma'am," Raine said, her tone sure.

Cat narrowed her eyes slightly. "I don't have clearance from your doctor yet."

Raine's lips twitched. "I know, ma'am, he's being a pain in the— sorry, ma'am."

Cat sighed. "Where you should be sorry," she said, her eyes sparkling with subdued humor, "is the part where you missed me telling you to call me Cat, and to stop calling me ma'am."

Raine's eyes widened. "But you're my supervisor."

"And I'm thirty-two friggin' years old, and while that may seem old to kids like you, it's not old enough to be a *ma'am* yet," Cat railed, then she grinned. "See my issues?"

"Yes, ma— Cat," Raine said, correcting herself mid-sentence.

"Very good," Cat said, smiling. "So what is your doctor saying is his concern?"

Raine sighed. "He said that he doesn't like my pulmonary function, he says that my levels were off during a stress test."

4

"So what is he recommending?"

"He wants me to do more cardio training, and he wants me to stay out of work for another month."

"And you don't want to do that, why?"

Cat knew that the department was paying her full salary while she was out, since she was injured on the job, so she knew money wasn't the factor.

"I can't sit at home anymore," Raine said, shrugging.

"Okay, that I understand. Well, I can't let you be in the field until he releases you. Jericho will have my head if I do that. But," she said, when Raine looked like she was going to argue, "you can work on cases here in the office."

Raine nodded, looking pleased by that option.

"So what do you do for cardio?"

Raine shrugged. "Run, mostly."

Cat nodded. "Well, you mentioned the dancing thing, which is why I asked. Jovi and I go to a cardio dance class at the gym we belong to…" She gave Raine a sidelong look. "Maybe you could check it out? It might be a little more interesting than running."

Raine smiled. "It sounds like it could be."

"Well, let me know if you're interested, I'll give you the address. Now, my next question," Cat said, narrowing her eyes again, "have you gone to any counseling about the accident?"

Raine instantly looked chagrinned.

"And that answers that question," Cat said, nodding. "Do you at least have family to talk to about what happened?"

"No, I don't have any family," Raine said.

Cat looked back at her, curious about the way she'd said it.

"No family?" Cat asked.

"None," Raine answered.

"Friends?"

"Well, I have you know… the team," Raine said.

"Uh…" Cat stammered. "But no other friends? Like non-cop friends? Or even other cop friends?"

"No," Raine said, shrugging, "I just haven't really had time."

Cat canted her head. "Explain that."

Raine drew in a breath. "When I joined the SO I found out that you could go farther faster if you had a degree, so I went back to school to get my bachelor's degree in criminal justice. I just finished it before I came to the task force."

"You got a bachelor's degree in three years?" Cat asked, surprised.

"Well… two actually," Raine said hesitantly. "But I already had my general education out of the way, so I just had to take the major specific classes."

"How did you have the general ed. out of the way?" Cat asked, sensing an underlying current to Raine's answers.

Raine hesitated, and Cat knew she hadn't been wrong about the current. Cat narrowed her eyes at the younger woman when she didn't answer. Raine saw the look, and knew she needed to just say it and get it over with.

"Because I completed my Bachelor of Fine Arts at Juilliard in New York," she rushed through the explanation, hoping against hope that Cat didn't ask any more than that.

It was obvious from the look on Cat's face that she wanted to ask questions, but Raine was relieved to note that she wasn't asking them. When Cat nodded, Raine closed her eyes for a moment, thanking fate for whatever hand it had just played in Cat's decision not to ask.

Cat was thinking that this girl was a whole mess of contradictions and mysteries. She was young, but she had not one but two degrees. Cat wasn't sure if she'd ever get the whole story out of her, but she could see that the last thing Raine wanted right now was for her to ask more questions. Cat decided to leave those questions for another time and place.

"Well, like I said, if you want to check out this cardio dance class, just let me know. The girl that teaches it is a former dancer, so it's pretty good."

"I think I'd really like to check it out," Raine said, nodding.

"Great," Cat said, scribbling an address on the pad in front of her and tearing off the sheet to hand to Raine. "Her classes are every weeknight at six thirty and on the weekends at ten a.m."

"So there's one every weeknight?" Raine asked.

"Yep," Cat said, nodding. "Jovi and I go most nights, so if you want to meet us there some night, we can get you a guest pass to check out the class."

Raine smiled. "That would be great!"

***

In Sacramento, California, Kashena Windwalker-Marshal sat smoking in her backyard. Her mind was going a mile a minute; she knew there were a lot of things to consider with what she'd heard today. She heard the back door open, and glanced over her shoulder. She grinned.

"LA huh?" she asked.

Sierra Youngblood-Marshal rolled her eyes. "Yes, I can't believe this!" she said, sounding flabbergasted.

Midnight Chevalier, the dynamic California Attorney General had come to Sacramento to meet with Sierra, who was the Chief Deputy Attorney General in charge of the Criminal Division. The meeting had been about the Los Angeles Attorney General's office. Midnight's statement was that the office was "a mess" and she'd asked Sierra if she would be willing to relocate to the Los Angeles area, at least temporarily, to take charge of the LA office for Midnight.

"Midnight wouldn't ask you to do it if she didn't need you there, right?" Kashena said, her deep blue eyes sparkling in amusement.

"I know," Sierra said, shaking her head, her long dark hair falling to her waist. Shifting it out of the way, she sat down in the chair next to Kashena's.

Kashena looked over at her wife of a year. "She trusts you."

"I know," Sierra said. "How are you feeling about this though?"

Kashena shrugged. "When I was down there, Jericho offered me a job, so…"

"She did?" Sierra asked, not completely surprised.

Kashena had recently been key to solving a case involving Jericho Tehrani, the Director of the Division of Law Enforcement, earning her the gratitude of not only the director, but from the Attorney General.

Kashena was half Ojibwa Indian and had inherited her grandmother's gift of premonitions, "the sight" as it was referred to by her people. It had been that particular gift that had helped not only the director, but almost two years before, the Attorney General herself. She'd been an integral part of saving the Attorney General's life.

"Yeah, so I guess that's what I'll be doing," Kashena said.

"What do you want to do about the house?" Sierra asked.

"Up to you," Kashena said. "It's your house, babe."

Sierra gave her a sour look. "It's our house."

"Uh-huh," Kashena murmured, not looking convinced.

"You're helping make the payment," Sierra said, putting her hands on her hips.

Kashena grinned, noting the gesture.

"Stop that," Sierra said, narrowing her eyes at her wife.

This only caused Kashena to start laughing.

"Kashena Windwalker-Marshal, if you don't stop I'm not going to talk to you anymore," Sierra said, grinning.

"Ohhh mom-move, pulling out the whole name," Kashena said, grinning again.

Sierra grimaced. "How do you think this is going to affect Colby?"

Kashena looked serious, and leaned back to take a long drag off her cigarette.

"I don't think it's going to be easy," she said, "but he is just getting ready to start high school so if any time is going to be good, this may be it."

Colby, Sierra's son through her previous marriage had turned thirteen six months before and was due to start high school in a month.

"That's true," Sierra said, nodding, then sighed. "I hate to take him away from his friends though."

"It can't be helped babe," Kashena said, reaching over to touch Sierra's hand. "He's a smart kid, and outgoing, he won't have any problem making new friends."

Sierra nodded. "I know you're right," she sighed.

Kashena smiled fondly at her wife. Sierra was a good mother. Having been through so much with her divorce from Colby's father, it was like she was always trying to make up for the fact that his father wasn't there anymore.

Jason, a Marine, had been verbally abusive to his wife for years. Unfortunately, he'd become physically abusive when he'd sensed that he was losing control over his usually docile wife when Kashena had come into the picture. He hadn't known that Sierra had known Kashena from many years before in college, and that Kashena had been the woman that had made Sierra realize she was attracted to women. Sierra and Kashena had met again when Kashena had been assigned as Sierra's bodyguard, they'd been unable to resist the pull that drew them together.

Jason had returned from an overseas deployment with an overactive sexual appetite that had driven him to rape his own wife when she wouldn't give him sex. That had been the final straw for Sierra who'd only been staying with him for their son's sake. Jason had become enraged when Sierra had decided to divorce him, even striking her in front of Kashena, which had gotten him arrested. Since he'd also assaulted Kashena at the time of the incident, he'd gotten a fairly long prison sentence.

Fortunately, Colby had taken to Kashena right away when Sierra and he moved in with her the night after the incident with Jason. He'd learned that Kashena had also been a Marine, like his father, and that Kashena would protect his mother with her life if necessary. It had been that knowledge that had earned Kashena a ten-year-old boy's respect. It had been her treatment of him since that time that had earned her his love.

"It'll be okay," Kashena told Sierra, reaching up to touch her cheek.

Sierra smiled, softly, hoping Kashena was right.

Later that night, she found out when they talked to Colby about it during dinner.

"Los Angeles?" Colby asked.

"Yes," Sierra said, nodding, looking over at Kashena worriedly.

"It's not your mom's choice," Kashena said. "The AG has asked her to do it."

Colby looked over at Kashena, then looked back at his mother.

"Well, this totally sucks," Colby said angrily.

"I know, honey, but—" Sierra began.

"No you don't know, Mom, you don't get it at all!" Colby shouted.

"Colby…" Kashena said, her tone cautionary.

11

Colby immediately looked contrite. "I'm sorry, Mom," he said, lowering his eyes.

"Honey, I know this sucks, okay? I do. I just really don't have a choice right now," Sierra said.

"Okay," Colby said, sounding supremely unhappy.

Later that evening Kashena was once again in the backyard smoking, when Colby walked outside. She glanced over at him as he moved to sit down next to her.

"I'm sorry about earlier," he said.

Kashena nodded. "It's okay to be upset, Colby," she said. "It's just not okay to be disrespectful to your mother in the process."

"I know," he said.

"She's earned your respect, Col," Kashena said, her tone calm.

He drew his breath in, blowing it out slowly. Living with Kashena had taught him a lot about what it meant to be not only respectful, but what his responsibilities were as a man. He had a lot of respect for his stepmother. She had always treated him with respect, and all she expected in return was that same consideration. She would actually tolerate some disrespect from him, but would never tolerate him being disrespectful to Sierra. To him it proved how much she loved his mother, and it was that kind of thing that made Colby love Kashena. He remembered how his father had treated his mother. He'd been there when Jason had struck Sierra and had been terrified. It had been Kashena who'd stopped his father from hurting his mother and him, and it had been Kashena who'd made sure that he never hurt them again, by having him arrested.

"Do we really have to move to LA?" he asked.

"Right now," Kashena said, "yes we do. The Attorney General is your mom's boss and if she says she needs your mom in LA, that's what your mom needs to do."

"What about you?" Colby asked.

Kashena smiled. "It looks like I'll be working for the Division of Law Enforcement down there."

"Like the work you do here?"

Kashena was part of Midnight Chevalier's bodyguard detail when she was in Sacramento. She was also in charge of security in all of the Attorney General's offices throughout California.

"No," Kashena said, "I'd be running a task force down there."

"What kind of task force?" Colby asked.

"Not totally sure yet," Kashena responded. "I just have an offer from the Director of the Division of Law Enforcement, just not all the details yet."

"What about Baz?" Colby asked, referring to Kashena's best friend, Sebastian Bach who worked with her in the AG's security office.

Kashena grinned, appreciating the fact that Colby was worried about her best friend too.

"Actually, she offered Baz a job too, so…"

"So, is this that lady you helped a few months ago?" Colby asked.

"Yes, she's the director."

"Cool."

"Look, Col," Kashena said, looking over at her stepson. "We will do everything we can to make this transition easier on you, but I need you to make this as easy on your mom as you can, okay? She's under a lot of strain right now, and whether she admits it or not, she's worried about moving as much as you are."

Colby drew in a breath, nodding. He knew Kashena was truly asking him to help out, and he appreciated the fact that she treated him like his feelings mattered. He knew that wasn't always how parents were, and he was glad that he had the parents he did.

**

Jason Thorn sat in his cell in Folsom prison. It was dark on the block, because lights out had been hours before. He was sharpening the toothbrush he'd bought from the canteen. As he did, his eyes narrowed in the dark as he pictured what he planned to do when he got that dyke bitch in his grasp. In his anger his hand slipped and he felt the tip of the sharpened edge go into his hand. The pain was, in some perverse way, pleasure to him. Even the feeling of his own blood dripping from the wound felt good. He imagined it being her blood, she was going to pay for what she'd done, one way or the other.

**

Natalia Marquez was talking to one of her classmates as she left the lecture hall. She'd just said goodbye to the person she'd been talking to, and didn't see Julie until she almost ran into her. Pulling up short, she stepped back seeing who was in her path. She immediately looked around her, hoping that there were other people around. There weren't and no one was paying any attention to them.

"Why are you here?" she asked Julie.

Julie, a very butch lesbian, and Natalia's former girlfriend, tried her most winning smile. "You know you want to see me," she said, winking.

Natalia looked back at Julie, her look far from inviting.

"Are you screwing one of your little groupies now? Is that it?" Julie asked sharply.

Natalia stepped back again at the venom in Julie's tone.

"I'm not seeing anyone," Natalia said, holding her books with crossed arms in front of her chest, like a shield.

"But they're all panting after you now, aren't they?" Julie said, her tone snide.

"No one is panting after me." Natalia said.

"Don't fuckin' lie to me!" Julie said. "I see those cunts after you all the time!"

Julie was referring to the girls in Natalia's cardio dance class. It was true, there were girls in the class that seemed quite dedicated to not only the class, but the beautiful instructor as well. But Natalia had never let any of them think she was interested. It wouldn't have been appropriate as she'd been dating Julie at the time. It was for that reason that Julie was particularly sensitive about them now. Not that she hadn't been absolutely fanatical about keeping them away from Natalia, prior to their break up seven months earlier, but it had never been due to Natalia's behavior.

"I need to go," Natalia said, trying to move past Julie.

"You need to stay here and talk to me," Julie said, grabbing Natalia's arm roughly.

Natalia winced as Julie's strong fingers bit into her skin. "You're hurting me."

"You're not listening to me," Julie said, her tone heated. "If you'd just listen to me…"

"Julie!" Natalia cried as Julie increased the pressure on her arm.

Julie let her go, stepping back and shaking her head. "See? This is what you make me to do. You make me so crazy, I just want you back, but you won't listen!"

Natalia stayed silent, knowing that nothing she said to Julie would matter. It had been that way for a long time now, and it had been what had finally broken them up; that and Julie's increasingly violent behavior toward her.

"And what the fuck was up with all those dykes showing up to protect you? Huh? Why'd you do that?"

"I didn't," Natalia said, forgetting herself for a moment.

Julie was referring to an incident six months before. A group of women who came to her class regularly, as well as their butch girlfriends, had shown up at the gym when they'd heard that Julie was harassing her. She hadn't asked them to do so, in fact she'd been quite surprised by the show of support for her. Surprised and very touched.

"Sure, right," Julie said, sarcastically. "Course they all probably want to fuck you too, so that's no surprise."

"They're all either married or close to it," Natalia said, feeling the need to defend her friends even to Julie.

16

"That don't mean dick," Julie said dismissively.

"Julie, I need to get to my next class," Natalia said, trying to keep her voice calm.

"I said we need to talk!"

"Okay! But not here, okay?" Natalia said, willing to say anything to get away from Julie at that moment.

"Then when?" Julie asked.

"Soon."

Julie's eyes narrowed instantly. "You're just trying to get rid of me."

"No, I just don't know what my schedule looks like right now," Natalia said, trying to think fast.

"I don't care about your schedule," Julie said, taking a menacing step toward her again. "This is important."

"Okay, okay," Natalia said, holding her hand up, "how about tonight? At Ed's?"

Julie nodded. "What time?"

"Seven?"

"Okay, I'll be there."

"Great, I'll see you then," Natalia said, moving to get past Julie again.

Julie reached out and grabbed her again, pulling her in to kiss her roughly. Natalia had to keep herself from pushing Julie away, knowing it would only make her mad. She smiled up at Julie, then turned and hurried to her next class, pausing outside the door to regain her composure.

***

Raine pulled her sapphire-blue Honda Shadow up to the address Cat had given her for the dance class. She turned the bike off and sat back to observe the people walking into the gym for a few minutes, noting the varied clientele. As she sat there she noticed a deep red Dodge Challenger pull in a few cars away. She was surprised when she saw Jericho Tehrani, the Director of the Division of Law Enforcement get out and a blond woman get out of the passenger's side. *The director drives a car like that?* Raine thought to herself. She'd heard that Jericho was a pretty cool person, but she still wouldn't have expected her to drive that kind of car. This was the first time she'd seen the director.

Jericho Tehrani was fairly tall at five foot ten inches. She had very tanned skin, with long black hair that she had in a ponytail. She wore jeans, cowboy boots and a black polo shirt with the DLE logo on it. The girl with her was smaller and dressed in gym clothes; baby blue capri leggings and a white tank top with white tennis shoes. Jericho's arm was around the girl's shoulders and they were talking as they walked into the gym. Raine watched them go in, unable to take her eyes off of them. It seemed like she was seeing a lot of lesbian couples lately.

Getting off her bike, she hooked her helmet to the clip on the side, locking it on. As she did, she saw a blue Nissan 370Z pull into the lot, which she recognized as Catalina's car. She waited for Cat to get out, and noted that Jovina was with her.

Cat smiled. "You made it!"

"Yep," Raine said, smiling, then she nodded respectfully at Jovina. "Ma'am."

"Please call me Jovina, or Jo," Jovina said.

"Another person that doesn't like ma'am," Raine said.

"I'm too young," Jovina replied.

"Got it," Raine said, nodding.

Inside, they signed Raine in and then Cat showed her where she could change and where the dance room was. Raine nodded, setting her backpack down on a bench in the changing room. She emerged ten minutes later wearing black capri leggings as well as a black tank that conformed to her slim dancer's body. On her feet she wore black Nike's with purple and lime-green accents; it was the only color to her outfit. It was very different from the other women that attended the class who wore riots of color usually in an effort to outdo each other.

Raine walked toward the dance room, seeing Cat and Jovina waiting for her. They were standing with Jericho Tehrani and her girlfriend. As she walked up, Raine inclined her head respectfully to Jericho.

"Ma'am," she said.

Jericho grinned immediately glancing at Cat.

"Raine, this is Jericho, and call her that if you don't want to hear the same kind of crap you've been getting from me for the last two weeks," she said with a wink, then she gestured to the blond. "And this is Zoey Cabbott."

Raine extended her hand to Zoey, smiling.

"Zoey, Jericho, this is Deputy Raine Mason, she's on my task force."

Jericho nodded. "You were injured recently," she said, having read the report. "How are you doing?"

Raine was surprised that the director knew about her injury. "I'm good, ma'am... I mean Jericho," she said correcting herself with a grin.

"I told her about Natalia's class," Cat said. "She's still working on the medical release."

Jericho nodded. "Natalia will whip pretty much anyone into shape."

Then she nodded toward the door as Natalia came into the gym. "Speak of the devil..."

Natalia was dressed in black capri leggings with bright green around the lower quarter of the legs, and a matching bright green top. Over it she wore a black and bright green accented long sleeved zip up jacket, and matching shoes. As always, she wore matched eyeshadow, with her usual black liner framing her chocolate-brown eyes. She also had her long black hair back in a ponytail. Her smile was radiant as always.

"Raine," Cat said, putting her hand to the woman's back, "this is Natalia. Natalia, this is Raine, she's a member of my unit."

"It's great to meet you," Natalia said, smiling as her eyes took in Raine. She held the look for an extra few moments, which had Raine feeling flustered suddenly.

"I... you too," Raine stammered as she nodded, not understanding why she was suddenly tongue tied.

"I better get in there. Don't be late," she chided to Cat and Jovina, and then winked at Raine, "you either."

A few minutes later, Cat guided Raine into the class. Raine took up a position in the back, since she had no idea what she was in for, she didn't want to get in anyone's way. As the class filled up, Raine noticed that Jericho had been joined by a few other women at the side of the room. They were all watching the class. Cat and Jovina had been joined by Zoey, two other blond women and another woman with black hair with purple streaks. They all stood on the same line together. Raine guessed from the way they talked that they knew each other.

As the class started, Raine concentrated on watching Natalia's steps. She quickly picked up on the steps as well as the rhythm of the class. She really enjoyed the class; Natalia was definitely a good dancer, her moves were almost hypnotic. Raine also noted that Natalia's musicality was uncanny, and her ability to match moves to the changes in music was incredible. It was far from the type of experience she'd expected to have in a gym class. Before long she was fully involved in the class. She didn't notice the looks she was getting as she danced. She was able to easily perform moves that others in the class had a hard time with, and she did so with the grace of the dancer that she was. She also didn't notice the conversation going on at the side of the room.

Jericho had been joined by Quinn Kavanaugh and Skyler Boché.

"Holy shit," Jericho said, seeing the way Raine moved.

"Got that right," Quinn agreed. "She's picking it up damned fast, didn't you say this was her first class?"

"That's what Cat said," Jericho said.

"No one picks it up that fast. Nat's moves are way too complicated for regular people..." Skyler said. She'd observed the class the longest out of all of them.

21

"And the other girls are noticing…" Quinn said, as she saw yet another longtime attendee of the class throw a dirty look in Raine's direction.

"Trouble brewing there…" Skyler said.

Julie was right about the "groupies" in Natalia's class. Many of the girls were simply so dedicated to Natalia that they got jealous of anyone new. There were a couple of girls in the class that did have romantic feelings toward Natalia, but for the most part it was more of a territorial thing. They definitely didn't like this new girl coming in and showing them all up, because it was also obvious that Natalia was noticing this new girl too.

Natalia had indeed noticed Raine, and not just because of her dancing; she'd been struck by the girls beautiful light blue eyes, and rich red hair. Before the class had begun, Natalia had noticed the way that Raine was stretching, using ballet foot positioning to stretch her calves and leg muscles. When the class started, Natalia had also watched how she picked up the steps extremely quickly. In Raine, Natalia recognized a fellow dancer; that was the only explanation for her being such a quick study. It also explained the slim and well-toned body the girl had.

Midway through the class, Cat noticed that Raine was breathing heavily. During a water break, she walked over to her.

"Take it easy," Cat told her, "you're pushing too hard."

Raine nodded as she wiped her face with a towel. "I really like the class," she said, out of breath.

Natalia called everyone back to the floor and the class began again. The next few songs were what the class deemed as 'killer,' which meant they were particularly strenuous.

22

At the side of the room, Jericho noted that Raine was breathing heavily and her face was also getting flushed. She knew the injuries that the girl had sustained in the explosion of the lab, so she knew that her lungs weren't likely to be completely healed.

"Not good..." Jericho muttered.

"What?" Quinn asked.

Jericho nodded toward Raine. "She was injured in an explosion six months ago. She's not at full strength yet and she's pushing it."

Quinn nodded, watching the girl as she moved. Her protective instincts, which would measure off the charts if anyone had bothered to measure them, kicked in. She started to move closer to the dance floor, keeping her eye on the girl. Raine missed a couple of steps, something she hadn't done previously. That had Quinn stepping up to the edge of the floor. She caught Cat's glance back at Raine, and as Quinn turned her head back to Raine, she started to fall. Lunging forward, Quinn caught her, and lifted her easily to carry her over to a bench nearby. Raine was unconscious. Everyone in the class stopped.

Cat ran over to where Quinn had set Raine down and was checking her pulse. Quinn looked up at Cat as she ran up.

"Her pulse is racing, but it's already calming down," Quinn told Cat.

"Damnit, I knew she was overdoing it, I told her not to push it..." Cat said, shaking her head.

"She okay?" Jericho asked from beside Quinn.

"Yeah," Quinn said, nodding.

The other women in the class were crowding around to see what had happened which was quickly raising the temperature in that area. Cat turned around, gesturing for everyone to back up.

"Back up ladies, everything's okay," she said, using her cop voice.

Natalia made her way through the group looking worried. She'd already grabbed a cool, wet cloth and put it on Raine's forehead.

"She's okay? Are you sure?" Natalia asked anxiously.

"She just overdid it," Cat told Natalia.

Raine came to, opening her eyes which looked even lighter than normal. She saw all the faces hovering above her.

"What…" she started to say.

"You passed out," Jericho said.

"I… oh…" Raine said. She blinked slowly, then she touched the bench under her. "How?" she asked, obviously perplexed.

"Quinn caught you," Cat said. "She has a major white knight complex."

"Shut it," Quinn muttered in her Northern Irish accent.

"I… thank you," Raine said, looking at Quinn.

"No worries," Quinn said, her smile warm.

"Everybody back to class!" Natalia said then, gesturing to one of the girls, a fellow instructor, to lead the class.

She looked over at Cat. "Let's get her to the office," she said. Looking down at Raine, she reached down to touch her cheek. "Can you stand?"

Raine blinked a couple of times, and then nodded as she moved carefully to sit up. Her vision swam, so she shook her head as she lay back down.

"Just give me a minute," she said, doing her best to gather her strength.

"Here, let me," Jericho said impatiently, moving to scoop the girl up.

Natalia lead the way to the office, where there was a couch. It would be much more comfortable than the bench in the dance room. Jericho gently laid Raine down there, giving her a reassuring smile. Raine was thinking it wasn't probably every day that a deputy sheriff got carried around by the Director of the Division of Law Enforcement; she knew it was a first for her.

Everyone left the room, except for Cat and Natalia.

"How ya doing?" Cat asked after a few minutes.

Raine nodded, her eyes still closed.

Natalia moved to sit on the floor next to Raine's head, pressing a bottle of Gatorade into her hand.

"Drink this, mija," Natalia said, using a Spanish term of endearment.

Raine nodded again, lifting the bottle to her lips and drinking.

"Esto no esta bien, miel," Natalia said then, reverting to her native language in the stressful situation.

"It's okay, I'm okay," Raine said, in response, surprising the dance instructor.

"You speak Spanish?" Natalia asked.

"I understand it," Raine said, nodding.

Natalia smiled, unaccountably pleased that this woman understood her language.

"Spanish Harlem," Cat said, looking over at them.

Raine lifted her arm up, her index finger up in a *got it* signal.

"You lived in Spanish Harlem?" Natalia asked, surprised.

"Grew up there," Raine answered.

"Oh," Natalia said, nodding.

Raine finally moved to sit up, suddenly feeling embarrassed at the situation.

"I'm gonna go," Raine said, as she stood up.

Cat noted the flush to her cheeks, and guessed that she was embarrassed now. She nodded, watching Raine head out of the room. Natalia stared after her, looking confused.

"She's embarrassed," Cat told her.

"Why?" Natalia asked.

"Fainted the first day of class?" Cat said.

"Oh…" Natalia said, nodding.

She was still trying to equate the pretty red head with Spanish Harlem and not having a lot of luck.

Chapter 2

Half an hour later, after a shower and a change of clothes, Raine found Quinn and Jericho standing near her bike. Cat's vehicle was now parked next to her bike, and she was leaning on the hood. They were apparently waiting for her.

Raine steeled herself as she walked over to her bike.

"Raine, this is Quinn," Cat said, nodding at the woman with the tattoos and short red hair. "She's the one that kept you from becoming one with the floor this evening."

Raine nodded at Quinn. "Thank you."

"S'okay," Quinn said, narrowing her eyes slightly at the girl. "Are you sure you're okay to ride now though?"

Raine looked back at her, blinking a couple of times, her look perplexed.

"You did just lose consciousness," Jericho put in.

Raine looked at Jericho, shaking her head. "I'm fine, ma'am."

"How about," said the woman Cat said was named Devin, "we all go have some dinner, and that way we know you're okay before you get onto that thing," she said, gesturing at Raine's bike.

"But how…" Raine began, gesturing helplessly at the bike.

"You can ride with me," Jericho said, "and I'll bring you back after dinner."

"I'm really fine, ma'am," Raine said, feeling a bit like she was being cornered.

"Mira, what's happening?" Natalia asked, walking up to the group.

"We're trying to convince Deputy Mason that she should eat something before she tries to ride her bike home," Quinn said.

"Bien, you should, mija," Natalia said, nodding.

"You should come too," Cat said, grinning at Natalia.

"Ay! Always trying to get me to eat!" Natalia responded, laughing.

"'Cause we're not convinced you do," Jericho said, winking at Natalia.

"Carina, save me," Natalia said, grabbing Raine's arm jokingly.

Raine was just happy to have the focus off of her for the moment, so she nodded.

"I'll bring Miss Raine," Natalia said, rolling the 'r' in her name. "A dónde?" she asked, wanting to know where.

"Mary's?" Quinn suggested.

"Sounds good," Cat said, and the others nodded agreement.

"We'll see you there," Natalia said, taking Raine's arm to steer her toward her car, a little red Honda Civic.

In Natalia's car, Raine did her best to relax, but things just seemed to keep happening that evening that she had no control over and it was making her feel tense. Natalia started the car, and glancing over at Raine, she could sense that the other woman was tense, she just didn't understand why. As she backed out of the parking space, she purposely turned her usually-loud music down, glancing a couple of times over at Raine.

"Que está pasando?" Natalia asked after a couple of minutes of silence from Raine. Asking what was happening in Spanish.

Raine looked over at Natalia. "I'm sorry," she said, shaking her head. "Things are just too… too much right now."

"Too much?" Natalia repeated. "Por que?" she asked, *Why?*

Raine drew in a deep breath, blowing out as she shook her head. "I don't really know. I just feel like too much is happening."

Natalia looked over at her again. "Is this too much?" Natalia asked, gesturing to the car around them.

Raine looked around her, then shook her head. "I just…" she said, then shrugged, unable to describe the feeling.

Natalia pulled up to a red light and looked over at her again. She turned off her stereo and reached across the center console. She took Raine's hand in hers rubbing her thumb over top of Raine's hand slowly.

"Try something for me, mija," Natalia said softly. "Close your eyes."

Raine looked at her perplexed.

"Por favor para mi?" she said, saying "please, for me."

Raine drew in a breath and then nodded, closing her eyes.

"Ahora, take twenty slow deep breaths," Natalia said, glancing up at the light that was still red.

She watched as Raine did as she asked, and could immediately see the tension leaving her body. Natalia didn't let Raine's hand go, continuing to smooth her as she breathed. The light turned green and Natalia continued to drive toward the restaurant in West Hollywood, her hand still in Raine's.

Raine was shocked by how different she felt. She felt like her strain was just melting away. When she'd done the twenty breaths, she opened her eyes and looked over at Natalia.

"That's amazing," she said, thinking that Natalia was a miracle worker. "How did you know that would help?"

Natalia winked. "I understand stress."

Raine shook her head. "It's never been that easy before."

"This happens a lot?" Natalia asked.

"Sometimes."

"Then remember that trick."

"I will," Raine said, smiling, "thank you."

"De nada," Natalia said, glad she'd been able to help.

They were both quiet for a while, then Raine looked over at Natalia. "I really like your class."

Natalia smiled. "Gracias, I'm glad."

"Cat said you were a professional dancer?" Raine said. "Why'd you stop?"

"I was in a car accident," Natalia replied. "I did all the therapy, but esta hecho," she said, indicating that her career was just done.

"I'm sorry," Raine said, sadly.

"Esta bien," Natalia said, "I'm okay."

After a few more minutes, Natalia looked over at Raine. "Que estaba pasando in class tonight?" she asked, wanting to know what had happened with Raine in class.

Raine bit her lip, looking a bit abashed. "I was in an accident a few months ago and my lung function isn't back up to a hundred percent yet."

"And you were working that hard? Estas loca?" Natalia asked, wanting to know if she was crazy.

Raine chuckled. "No, I was just really enjoying the class, and let myself overdo it."

"Well, don't do that again," Natalia said, "me estustaste!" telling Raine that she'd freaked her out.

"I'm sorry, I didn't mean to scare you or anyone else," Raine responded.

"Si, but don't do it again," Natalia said, shaking her head. "Niña loca!"

Raine grinned, not used to having anyone be worried about her. She'd been on her own for so many years that she had no idea what to do when other people were concerned for her. It was a source of anxiety for her.

At the restaurant the group sat discussing Raine before she and Natalia got to the restaurant.

"Should she really be back on duty yet?" Jericho asked.

"She's not on full yet," Cat said. "I've still got her on medical light duty."

Jericho nodded. "I can see why."

"I know," Cat said, her lips twitching.

"You couldn't know she was going to overdo it like that, babe," Jovina pointed out, knowing that Cat was blaming herself for Raine's collapse. "In fact you told her to take it easy, she just didn't listen."

"Did you see how fast she picked that stuff up?" Skyler asked.

"She graduated from Juilliard in New York," Cat said.

"What?" Jericho exclaimed, and everyone else made some similar exclamation.

Cat nodded, then shrugged. "Not sure why she became a cop or why she moved here."

"Did you ask?" Quinn asked.

"I don't think she wanted me to," Cat said. "She got pretty nervous when she admitted the part about Juilliard. I didn't want to scare her off."

"I understand that," Devin said, giving Skyler a sidelong look.

Skyler caught the look and closed her eyes grimacing slightly. Devin knew all too well how rough it could be trying to get to know someone who had a story they didn't want to share. Skyler, who'd been involved in a crash while serving in Iraq, had serious post-traumatic stress disorder and it had taken a lot of pain and work to get healthy again. It had also almost cost their relationship and they both now fully understood not to push people on their secrets.

The rest of the group nodded, as most of whom knew the general facts of their story.

"Think she's family?" Quinn asked.

The term "family" was used by gays to indicate people of their own kind.

Cat shrugged. "Got me. I mean, she could definitely be a soft butch, but I haven't seen any evidence of it. She definitely hasn't said anything about it."

Quinn winked at Xandy who'd discovered she was gay when she'd become infatuated with her very butch bodyguard.

"Maybe she hasn't realized it yet?" Quinn said.

"Doesn't matter," Cat said. "She needs friends."

"She doesn't have any?" Jericho asked, surprised.

"She says she hasn't had time," Cat said, not looking convinced with that answer.

"Well, she can join our happy little band," Zoey said.

"I second that motion," Xandy said.

"Here, here," Jerry said.

"So what do you think was up with Natalia tonight?" Jericho asked.

"With the sleeves?" Cat said.

"Yeah, I noticed that too," Quinn said, nodding.

"Think Julie is still being a problem?" Jovina asked.

"I think we should try to find out," Zoey said.

"Yeah, definitely," Jericho said.

They'd had a passive-aggressive meeting with Julie at the gym six months before, trying to convince her that leaving Natalia alone was in her best interest.

During class that evening, they'd noticed that Natalia had been wearing a long-sleeved shirt even though it was mid-summer in LA. It was very suspicious. And it led everyone to believe that perhaps Julie hadn't taken the hint.

When they arrived, Natalia and Raine were escorted out to the patio where the rest of the group was seated. Cat, Jericho, Skyler and Quinn were smoking.

"Make sure you stay in the no-smoking section," Cat said, grinning at Raine.

"That's upwind there," Jericho said, gesturing to the left side of the table.

"You should be sitting there too," Zoey told Jericho.

"But then I can't smoke," Jericho replied.

"I think that's her point, Jerich," Quinn said.

"Doc said, I was good to go," Jericho said.

"He never said that smoking was okay," Zoey said, giving Jericho a narrowed look.

"He never said it wasn't," Jericho countered.

Most of the group started to chuckle.

"Sorry," Cat said to Raine and Natalia, "this is an ongoing dispute."

"She had a lung injury a few months ago too," Zoey said.

"It's been almost a year now," Jericho said.

"Doesn't seem like that," Jovina said.

"That's 'cause you weren't doing the physical therapy to get back here," Jericho said, winking at Jovina.

"Ah," Jovina said, smiling

Jericho looked over at Raine. "Take it from me," she said seriously, "You need to take your time getting back."

"Jerich went back too fast and just about wrecked that Challenger out there," Quinn told Raine.

"That's why you didn't want her riding her motorcycle," Natalia said, nodding as she finally understood.

"That and she looks like she could use a good meal," Skyler put in.

"Look who's talking," Devin said, poking her fiancée in the ribs.

Skyler winked at Devin. "You like me lean."

"Yeah, but you won't be winning any heavyweight championships anytime soon."

"The Army really beats the weight restrictions into ya, what can I say?" Skyler replied, shrugging.

"You were in the Army?" Natalia asked.

She'd met all these women, but didn't know a lot about their backgrounds. There wasn't a lot of time to socialize before the class and she was usually stuck talking to other women from the class after it was over.

Skyler nodded. "I was chopper pilot."

"She flies helicopters for LA Fire now," Devin said.

"Impresionante!" Natalia said, her eyes widening. Then she looked at Cat, then at Jericho and then Raine. "And you're all police officers?"

The three nodded.

"Jerry, I know you're la modela," she said, smiling. She and Jerry had talked at length about what Jerry wanted to work on to keep up her body.

"Devin, you work with computers, si'?" she asked.

Devin nodded, elbowing Skyler who had started to say something. Skyler just shook her head.

"Que dije?" Natalia said, looking confused. "What did I say?"

Skyler cleared her throat, looking at Devin who gave her a quelling look. Skyler then looked over at Natalia.

"She has a doctorate from MIT, and she likes to be called a hacker," Skyler said, grinning as her eyes sparkled mischievously.

"Mierda!" Natalia replied, shocked.

"Always gotta talk…" Devin said, giving Skyler a narrowed look.

"I'm proud of my girl, what can I say?" Skyler said, grinning unrepentantly.

"Hey, my girl has a doctorate too," Zoey said, her look saying, *So there!*

Natalia looked at Jericho. "You do?"

Jericho nodded. "In criminology."

"From Cambridge University," Zoey added.

"Do you all have degrees?" Natalia asked.

"Bachelor's in aeronautics," Skyler said, holding up her hand.

"Bachelor's in criminal justice," Cat said.

"Bachelor's in psychology, master's in women's studies," Zoey said.

36

"Soon to be a doctorate," Jericho added, winking at Zoey.

"School of hard knocks," Quinn said, grinning.

"That's in-house lifting, isn't it?" Cat asked with a grin.

"Funny," Quinn said, giving her a dirty look.

Cat noticed that Raine remained silent during the exchange. The girl had two degrees; she should have been bragging about them too, not keeping quiet. Cat figured she had her reasons, she just wasn't sure what they were.

The waitress came over then and handed them all menus. When drinks were ordered, Jericho announced that the first round was on her.

Everyone ordered beers or mixed drinks with relish. When the waitress got to Raine, she ordered bottled water. Everyone looked at her shocked.

Raine looked around seeing that everyone was staring at her. She shrugged. "I don't drink," she said simply, which had a few of the women looking at each other in surprise.

"Leave the kid alone," Jericho said. "Not everyone is a lush like us."

"Speak for yourself," Quinn said.

"You're from Northern Ireland," Xandy said, winking at her girlfriend. "By definition a lush."

There was a round of "ohs" but it easily distracted everyone from Raine. Cat noted the relief on the girl's face. Unfortunately, when the food showed up, once again the focus went back to Raine. Everyone else was eating burgers, fries, and any number of other fried foods, while Raine had ordered a seared ahi tuna salad.

"That looks… uh, healthy," Skyler commented.

"I didn't know Hamburger Mary's even made anything healthy," Devin said, surprised.

"Not much," Cat said, trying to figure Raine out and failing to do so.

"It looks good," Natalia said. She'd ordered a salad as well, but she was also sharing nachos with Zoey.

In the end, everyone figured out that Raine wasn't really good at getting poked at, so they made a point of not teasing her. Cat sensed that Raine was fairly intimidated by the group, although she did seem to enjoy the banter between the women, she just didn't get involved in it. She seemed to be more of an observer.

After dinner, they all walked out to the parking lot together. Everyone said goodbye to everyone else. Cat did a last check on Raine.

"Okay, you're sure you're good to get home?" Cat asked, although she hadn't seen any issues during dinner.

"I'm sure," Raine said, nodding.

"Okay, then I'll see ya tomorrow," Cat said. "Thanks Nat for taking her back to the gym."

"De nada," Natalia said, smiling at Cat.

The drive back to the gym was quiet for a little bit.

"You're not used to being around so many people, are you?" Natalia asked Raine.

Raine shook her head. "No, not really."

Natalia considered that for a long moment. "You seem… como se dice…? solitario, lonely?" she said, not sure if she was using the right word. "Kind of… triste, sad."

Raine looked over at Natalia, her light blue eyes considering, then she shook her head.

"No," she said, "I just… I'm not good at social situations." Then she added, "No saliente."

Natalia looked shocked once again, Raine's accent was perfect.

"I thought you only understood," Natalia said, her tone shrewd. "You are what my mother would call aguas profundas."

"Deep water?" Raine replied.

"Muy profundo," Natalia said, her look serious, but sad in a way that Raine didn't understand.

Back at the gym, Natalia got out of the car so she could grab her gym bag and move it to the front seat of her car. She surprised Raine by reaching up to hug her goodbye. Raine felt completely awkward but hugged the smaller girl back. Natalia watched as Raine climbed onto her bike, put her helmet and riding gloves on and started the bike with a rumble. She backed her car out, and waited for Raine to walk her bike back, and then watched as she put it in gear and rode off. Raine Mason definitely made an engaging figure on her motorcycle, dressed in jeans, a black leather riding jacket and black leather riding boots. The Honda Shadow was sleek and low with sapphire blue on the tank and wheel fenders. It was a difficult picture to erase from her mind as she drove home to her apartment in West Hollywood.

"How about Brentwood?" Sierra said, as she climbed into bed next to Kashena. It had been a week since they'd learned of the move to Los Angeles.

"Expensive," Kashena said. She was sitting on their bed reading a report.

Sierra looked back at her wife, a strikingly beautiful woman with long blond hair and deep sapphire-blue eyes. She wore black shorts and a gray tank top with the Marine logo on it, and her hair was up in a long ponytail.

"Not if we sell this house," Sierra said, gesturing around them.

"Are you sure you want to do that?" Kashena asked.

"I bought this house with him," Sierra said, moving to lay on her side and levering herself up on her elbow to look up at Kashena. "I want to buy something with you."

Kashena quirked a grin at her wife. "Okay…" she said. "But how much are we talking in Brentwood, hon?"

"We don't have to have something huge; it's just the three of us," Sierra said.

"And how much does *not huge* cost in Brentwood, babe?" Kashena asked, looking down at her wife.

Sierra moved to sit up, knowing she was likely going to have to catch Kashena when she fainted dead-away.

"Well," she said cautiously, "anything decent is going to run between one point eight and two…"

Predictably, Kashena's mouth dropped open.

"I'm sorry…" she said, blinking a couple of times, "is that one point eight million?"

"Yes, but wait, wait, wait," Sierra said, holding up her hands as Kashena started to laugh.

"Babe, we don't have that kind of money," Kashena said.

"Well, wait," Sierra said. "If we put down five hundred thousand, the payment would only be about seven thousand a month."

"You're insane," Kashena said. "I love you, but you're crazy."

"We make enough," Sierra said.

Kashena looked back at her wife. "Why do you want to live there?"

"Because it has a great school district, and it's a safe neighborhood."

Kashena looked back at her wife for a long moment with a pointed look.

"It's a really nice neighborhood too, you said so yourself," Sierra said.

"Yeah, for the people who make a lot more money than me," Kashena said.

"But it isn't just you, now, Kash…" Sierra said softly.

Sierra had a point. Kashena was so used to being the breadwinner in her relationships. Sierra, as a Chief Deputy Attorney General, actually made more money than she did. It was something Kashena wasn't used to and she still really hadn't made the adjustment.

Kashena blew her breath out, shaking her head. "I'm sorry, Sierra, you're right."

"I'd like to look there," Sierra said, putting her hand on Kashena's chest. "But if you don't like anything, or you feel like it's too much we can check out other areas, okay?"

Kashena smiled, knowing that Sierra was trying to keep her from freaking out completely, while also respecting that Kashena wasn't used to a partner that made more money than her. It was the nature of a lesbian with a butch personality to expect to provide for her partner. The fact that Sierra didn't need the support didn't change Kashena's desire to provide for her.

Kashena's reconciliation with the financial situation was that she was Sierra and Colby's protector. She took care of them. She also handled anything physical in the house, with Colby's assistance, because she was raising him to be a good man. If something broke, Kashena either fixed it or made the arrangements to have it fixed. She also handled all maintenance of the vehicles, and took care of the yard.

Sierra knew that Kashena was the best thing that had ever happened to her, and she loved her more than she could ever explain to anyone. What she did do, was try to be the best wife she could be, doing her best to support Kashena in every way possible. She also knew it meant that she'd sometimes need to compromise to keep Kashena from feeling inadequate as a provider. For what she got with Kashena, compared to what she got from her marriage to Jason, Sierra was willing to walk through fire.

Jason had been a Marine, like Kashena had once been but that was where the similarities between the two ended. Jason had been a foulmouthed, overly aggressive, sexual pig of a man. Kashena rarely cussed in front of Sierra, always speaking to her with respect and love. On the very rare occasions when they'd disagree about something, Kashena would take the time to explain her thinking and why she didn't agree with a situation. She rarely raised her voice and when she did it was usually at Colby, and always when he was doing something that she knew could hurt him.

One such time, he'd been standing on a ladder and over-reaching farther out than he should have been. Kashena had barked a short order to, "Stop! Look!" scaring both him and Sierra, but it had made an impression on Colby when he'd realized how dangerous his action had been. He'd been positioned over the pointed edges of the rod iron fence, and had he fallen, he would have been impaled and likely killed.

When it came to sex, Kashena was always respectful and in some instances downright reverent of Sierra. As was a butch lesbian trait, Kashena always made sure that Sierra was completely satisfied during their lovemaking. Fortunately, Sierra had such a sensual effect on Kashena, she was usually quite sated by their lovemaking. They were well matched sexually and it made Sierra feel very complete to know that she'd found someone like Kashena who understood her in every possible way. Kashena knew when she just needed to be held and told that everything would be okay. She also could sense when Sierra wanted to lock their bedroom door and be ravaged. Kashena was always happy to oblige. As far as Sierra was concerned, their relationship was perfect, and she wouldn't change a thing about it.

***

43

Natalia had been avoiding Julie for weeks again. She'd met her that night at the café as she said she would, but refused to take Julie back. Fortunately, Julie wasn't willing to cause a scene in public so she'd finally left, albeit really angry. Natalia had become quite grateful for the consistent presence of Cat, Jericho, Raine and the other ladies at her classes. It seemed to keep Julie in check, for the most part. The bruises on her arm the night she'd gone to dinner with the group had finally faded, and she'd been able to go back to the tank tops she was used to wearing for her classes. Thankfully her Latin skin didn't hold onto bruises long.

Raine had become a regular attendee of her class. Natalia had made a point of regularly checking on her, telling her to slow down if she felt Raine was over doing it. It hadn't taken long for the other girls in the class to become jealous.

On one such occasion, during a routine that called for the dancers to move backward at a fairly good pace, one of the girls had purposely crowded Raine. Natalia had seen it and had moved to correct the person, but she'd caught Raine's quick shake of her head. Cat had seen the move as well and found herself watching carefully to see how Raine handled things. The next time the routine called for a backward movement, Raine purposely didn't step back for the first step, and when the girl who'd crowded her earlier attempted it again, she ran into Raine's forearm and elbow. She had fallen forward, barely keeping herself from making facial contact with the floor. She'd snapped her head around to give Raine a dirty look. Raine's look had been pointed and essentially said, *Don't fuck with me.* The girl had limped off to the side of the dance floor, and that had been the last time she'd moved in on Raine.

"Nicely done…" Cat had said, from just behind Raine.

Raine had grinned, glancing back at Cat. "Not the first time I've dealt with a bully in a dance class."

Cat had laughed, nodding, she imagined that was true.

There'd been some smack talking after that, and three girls from the class had the temerity to follow her out to the parking lot. It was obvious they hadn't been informed that Raine was a police officer. Raine had walked over to her bike, with the three girls following her.

"Hey puta!" one of the girls snapped, pushing up to Raine.

Raine, who stood a good six inches taller than the Mexican girl and was by no means intimidated, quirked her lips in a grin.

"High school Spanish, really?" Raine had said her tone derogatory.

"What do you know about Spanish?"

"Probably a lot more than you," Raine had replied, canting her head, even as she kept the other two girls in her line of sight.

"I'm Mexican, stupida!"

"Y yo soy Americano, cual es tu punto?" Raine had said, her accent dead on.

"That means she's American, what's your point?" Natalia had said from behind them.

The girls had immediately looked repentant. "Nat, we're sorry," said the one who'd been trying to intimidate Raine. "She's just so gallito!"

"She's got a lot to be cocky about," Natalia said, winking at Raine. "She's the best dancer in the class. Mi estudiante numero uno," she said, *My number one student.*

The girls' mouths had dropped open in shock, they'd left and hadn't returned to class for a couple of weeks. When they did return they didn't even look at Raine again.

Natalia had gotten so used to seeing Raine in her class, she was surprised when she didn't come for a week. When another couple of days passed, she found it necessary to ask Cat about her. Cat hadn't been around much either.

"We've been killing it on a case, doing hours and hours in the office and then going out on raids," Cat said, looking chagrinned. "Last night she must have been too tired. She'd gotten into an accident when an impatient driver cut her off."

"Aye dios mio!" Natalia exclaimed. "Is she okay?"

Cat nodded. "Yeah, but she's probably not going to be here for a bit."

"Can I check on her?" Natalia asked, looking very worried.

"Sure," Cat said, glancing at Jovina who raised an eyebrow.

"Can you text me her address?" Natalia asked, noticing that everyone was waiting for her to start class.

"Will do," Cat said, nodding, and she and Jovina moved to get into one of the lines of the class.

Jovina grinned. "Oh my."

"Tell me about it," Cat muttered.

As it turned out, Raine lived down the street from where Natalia lived in Pasadena. It amazed Natalia that she'd never run into Raine in the area. Raine lived in a complex called Terraces at Paseo in Pasadena. It was a ten minute walk from Natalia's apartment complex, Villas of Pasadena. Walking through the lobby, Natalia could see that it was a nice upscale apartment complex. When she walked up to the door to the apartment she realized she was nervous. She knew it was silly, because she was simply checking on a friend, but her inner voice said, *Really? Is that all?* She pushed the voice away. That was just silly, she didn't even know if Raine was gay, let alone interested in her.

Lifting her hand she knocked on the door. She was shocked when a man answered the door, although she realized she shouldn't be, Raine was a beautiful girl. The man was tall and skinny with ratty dirty blond hair and dull brown eyes. He wasn't the least bit handsome; he was just plain more than anything. He wore a dirty white t-shirt and faded ripped jeans. His bare feet looked like they needed a good scrubbing.

"Hi, I came to see Raine," Natalia said, feeling stupid suddenly.

She had pictured Raine living alone, and being alone after her accident. Now she felt incredibly presumptive and foolish for her thoughts, she really didn't know anything about Raine Mason at all.

"She's in there," the man said, hooking his thumb toward a door in the apartment.

With that, the man walked away. Natalia walked into the apartment, glancing around. The apartment was nice, but sparsely furnished. As she walked toward the door the man had indicated to, she saw that he was lying on the couch watching TV and eating from a bag of fast food. He dropped ketchup on his shirt but didn't seem to notice. He also paid Natalia no more mind. Now she was confused.

47

She knocked lightly on the door, and hearing a muffled "Yeah?" from inside the room, so she opened the door. She immediately heard music and she saw a Bose speaker dock sitting on a nearby dresser. The music was soft, but definitely hip-hop top forty type stuff.

Raine sat on her bed, wearing black shorts and an army-green shirt that had a "LASO" badge on the right front pocket area. Her hair was in a coiled braid at the back of her head.

"Oh, hi," Raine said surprised. "I thought you were my roommate again, he keeps trying to foist his extra burger on me."

"Not hungry?" Natalia asked, stepping into the room and closing the door.

"Don't eat that stuff," Raine said.

"You don't eat hamburgers?" Natalia asked, her eyes looking around the room, then back over at Raine.

"Not from a fast food place, no."

"But you're not a vegetarian?" Natalia asked.

"No," Raine said, shaking her head. "Why are you?"

"I ate steak on my salad, remember?" Natalia said in answer.

"Oh, true," Raine said.

"Aye dios mio…" Natalia breathed as she stepped closer, seeing the bloody rash on Raine's left forearm.

Raine glanced at her arm, and shrugged casually. "It's just a little road rash."

"It looks painful," Natalia said, moving to lift Raine's arm to get a better look.

"I've had worse," Raine said.

48

"Que esto?" Natalia asked, wanting to know if Raine meant worse road rash than that.

"Oh yeah," Raine said. "You don't ride motorcycles without getting a few road rashes in your time."

"Mierda!" Natalia gasped. "There's more?" she asked, seeing Raine's thigh had a nasty looking bloody rash on it as well.

"The doctor left it uncovered like this?" Natalia asked, aghast at such lax behavior by a doctor.

She caught Raine's abashed look and gave the girl an admonishing one of her own.

"You didn't go to the doctor did you?" Natalia accused more than asked.

Raine didn't answer for a moment, then she made a sucking sound through her teeth. "I don't like doctors."

"No one likes doctors, mija," Natalia said, "but they can make sure there's no infection!"

"I can make sure of that," Raine said, shrugging.

"Como?" Natalia asked, her hands on her hips.

"By making sure it stays clean," Raine said, her tone sure.

"And how do you do that?" Natalia asked, not swayed by Raine's confidence.

Raine looked back at the other woman for a long moment. "By taking regular showers and washing it."

"Aye!" Natalia said, throwing up her hands in dismay. "That isn't enough!"

Raine grinned bemusedly at Natalia. She had to admit, it was nice that someone cared about her. Cat had asked her if she needed anything, but having someone just show up to check on her was kind of cool. Even if she was being a bit fussy about it, it was still nice.

She realized that Natalia was standing with her hands on her hips giving her the evil eye.

"What?" Raine asked, honestly perplexed. Natalia found herself smiling despite her ire at the girl for taking such poor care of herself. Raine had an innocence about her that was far too engaging. At that moment, her light blue eyes seemed to glow. *Like a halo*, Natalia thought to herself.

"Por el amor de dios!" Natalia muttered, saying, *Oh for God's sake*, as she shook her head. Then she gave Raine a pointed look. "Donde esta el bano?" she asked, wanting to know where Raine's bathroom was.

Raine tried not to grin as she pointed to the area behind where Natalia stood. She saw Natalia's eyes narrow dangerously, so she pressed her lips together to keep the grin from growing. Natalia all but marched toward the bathroom, and Raine could hear her going through cupboards.

"Do you have peroxide?" Natalia called.

"Probably," Raine said, not sure if she did or not.

"Where is the first aid kit?" was the next thing that was yelled.

"Um," Raine stammered.

Natalia's head poked around the corner of the wall as she looked down at Raine. "You don't have one?!" she exclaimed.

"No?" Raine replied, grimacing.

"Aye dios mio!" Natalia exclaimed, followed by a lot of muttering that Raine couldn't completely hear, but she did hear the words "policia" and "desprevenido" which meant police and unprepared.

By the time Natalia stalked back into the room, Raine was nearly in tears trying so desperately not to laugh. She had her hand in front of her mouth, her eyes shiny with the unshed tears of hysterical laughter. Once again Natalia narrowed her chocolate-brown eyes.

"I am buying you a first aid kit tomorrow!" she exclaimed, setting down the items she had in her hands in a huff.

It was all Raine could take. She began laughing, holding her hands up in front of her defensively when Natalia stepped towards her, but it only made Raine laugh harder.

When she finally regained control of herself, she could see that Natalia was also amused. What she didn't know was that Natalia found Raine's laugh absolutely delightful; it was the first time she'd heard the woman laugh so happily and it warmed her heart.

"Can I do this now?" Natalia asked, holding up a tube.

"Do what?" Raine asked suspiciously.

"I need to put this on the rash and then wrap it with this," Natalia said, holding up the tube and a roll of gauze respectively as she spoke.

"I like my idea better," Raine said, indicating with her hand that she meant what she was currently doing for the rash.

"Ya veo," Natalia said. "Que pena," she said, telling Raine that she could see that's what she wanted to do, but that was too bad.

Raine chuckled again.

"Do you realize how often you speak Spanish?" she asked Natalia, her head canted slightly.

Natalia looked taken aback by the question, and thought about it. Finally she shrugged. "Con usted, mucho."

"A lot with me," Raine repeated in English, her nose twitching. "Why?"

Natalia looked back at her for a long moment, her own look perplexed. "I don't know." she said honestly.

In truth, Natalia hadn't realized how much she was speaking Spanish to the other woman. She never spoke Spanish to an American unless she was angry or trying to teach them Spanish, like with some of the girls in the class. She wondered if she'd automatically counted Raine as a fellow Mexican because of her background and her ability to understand Spanish. In any case, it was definitely something to think about.

Natalia narrowed her eyes at Raine suspiciously. "You are avoiding the subject…"

Raine laughed softly. "I wasn't trying to, honestly, I was just curious about that."

"Well I am too," Natalia answered. "But I also want this," she said, gesturing to Raine's injured arm and leg, "to heal, so… Con tu permiso?" she asked, seeking permission.

Raine sighed mightily but nodded.

To Raine's surprise Natalia climbed up on the bed, kneeling to Raine's left side opening the tube of ointment.

"This might hurt," Natalia said, biting her lip in concern.

Raine nodded, smiling softly at the worry on Natalia's face.

"Esta bien," she said, telling Natalia it was okay.

Natalia smiled, hearing Raine's perfect accent again and marveling at it. She really wanted to know exactly how fluently Raine spoke Spanish. She knew it was likely going to drive her crazy.

As Natalia applied the ointment she noticed that Raine didn't even flinch. Her brown eyes looked up into Raine's.

"This doesn't hurt?" she asked, surprised.

Raine shrugged slightly. "It hurts, but it's not a big deal."

"But you're not reacting at all," Natalia said.

"That doesn't mean it doesn't hurt," Raine said.

"So when do you react?" Natalia asked, ever confounded by this woman.

"When something really hurts," Raine said, her eyes staring back into Natalia's.

Natalia gave her a sidelong look. "Si tu lo dices…" she said, saying, *If you say so,* but her voice trailed off indicating that she wasn't sure she believed that.

Raine's lips twitched in a quick smile, she had no way of knowing how baffling she was to Natalia.

When Natalia was all finished applying ointment to the rash, she carefully wrapped the gauze around Raine's arm and leg, while Raine patiently looked on, her eyes sparkling in amusement.

"There," Natalia said, nodding with finality.

"Feel better?" Raine asked.

"Si."

"Thank you," Raine said, her smile genuine.

"De nada."

Moving to sit next to Raine on the bed, she looked around the room. She saw that Raine wasn't big on decoration, in fact there was almost nothing decorative in the room at all. Her furniture was nice in a dark wood, but not in the least bit opulent or ornate. The walls were painted a soft gray, the plantation style blinds were uncovered and the comforter on the bed was plain navy blue cotton. There was also no television.

"No TV?" Natalia asked, surprised by that realization.

Raine shrugged. "Nope."

"You don't watch TV?"

"Not really, I listen to music more often," Raine said, gesturing to the Bose speaker.

"Ah, si," Natalia said. Her life was all about music too. "I always have to have a radio on."

"Me too," Raine said.

"It always drove Julie loca," Natalia said, making a face.

"Julie?"

"My ex-girlfriend," Natalia said. "I thought Cat would have told you about her."

Raine shook her head slowly, she hadn't even really been aware that Natalia was a lesbian.

"Oh," Natalia said, "well we broke up months ago."

Raine nodded, not sure what to say at that point. Finally she asked, "She didn't like music?"

Natalia drew in a deep breath, blowing it out in a sigh. "Well, a lot of what I listen to is the kind of music I use in class, and she hated my class, so…"

Raine was shocked. "She hated your class?"

"Well, mostly she hated the girls in the class."

"Why?"

Natalia looked back at Raine for a long moment, trying to determine if she was serious in her question. She could see that she was indeed serious.

"Because a lot of them are interested in me," she said with a shrug, completely free of ego.

"Oh…" Raine said, once again shocked. It made the invasion of her space and the aggressive women in class make much more sense now; they thought Raine was interested in Natalia.

Natalia looked back at Raine, her look amazed. "You didn't know that I'm gay, did you?"

Raine shook her head.

"Does it bother you?" Natalia felt the need to ask.

"No," Raine said, "I just didn't really realize it."

Natalia smiled, once again astounded by the contradictions to this woman.

"But we're still amigas, right?" Natalia asked, wanting to know if they were still friends.

Raine laughed. "How could we not be? You just put icky gooey stuff all over my leg and arm."

Natalia laughed too. It was definitely an interesting night.

Chapter 3

"I love it," Sierra said, her eyes bright.

They were standing by a pristine pool, on the second level of the backyard of a house in a canyon near San Vicente Mountain Park. The house was a decent size hacienda-style home with four bedrooms. It had a lot of amenities that Kashena had been surprised by, such as a newly remodeled kitchen, the pool, and even a small creek running through the backyard. The 2,500-square-foot home sat on acre of land, practically unheard of in this part of town. In addition to the pool there was a barbecue area. It was definitely the house for entertaining. The price tag wasn't extreme, still more than Kashena would have ever dreamed of paying for a house, but they'd gotten a fairly quick offer for Sierra's house that would net them a tidy sum, plus what Kashena had in the bank from selling her house a year before. They could make a sizeable down payment and the monthly payments wouldn't be too difficult.

There was a charter high school just down the road, conveniently located on Kashena and Sierra's way to work. The drive was a significant hour each way, which was a factor, but since they would drive together most days it wasn't too much of a hardship. The house wasn't in Brentwood, but the privacy and land it had made up for that. It had been the first house they'd seen that Sierra had been completely over the moon about.

"Then let's make an offer," Kashena said, smiling.

"Yay!" Sierra said, throwing her arms around Kashena happily.

* * *

Raine shocked Cat by showing up for work the day after her accident.

"How did you get here?" she asked, knowing that Raine's bike was in the shop for repairs from the accident.

"Bus," Raine answered simply.

Cat stared back at the girl in shock. "Okay, but I'll drive you home."

"Ma'am…" Raine started to protest, shaking her head.

"I'm not asking, deputy," Cat said, her tone no-nonsense, causing the other members of the task force to grin.

"Okay," Raine said docilely, as she made her way over to her desk.

The other five members of the task force had agreed that they very much liked their new boss. Catalina Roché knew her business; she was good at giving direction as well as taking in information. She didn't try to act like a know-it-all, she was willing to listen and learn from all the members of her team. It was refreshing. The previous manager had been nearly useless. He'd been biding his time until he retired and everyone knew it. Whereas, Cat, liked to kick ass and take names. It had been a great change for the unit. It had also been why Raine had been afraid Cat would get rid of her, she'd been afraid she didn't know enough to stay.

"I can't believe you took the bus, little one," Aiden "Papa Bear" said to her as she walked past his cubicle.

"What's wrong with the bus?" Raine asked.

"It's not a smart way for a cop to travel," Aiden said.

"I turn my badge around and make sure I cover my weapon," Raine said.

"Doesn't matter," Aiden said. "If you're made for a cop you're not safe," Aiden responded, sounding very fatherly.

Raine drew in a breath and blew it out slowly, nodding her head. She already had so much on her mind, this was just one more thing. She'd been awake half the night, tossing and turning. Finally, at four o'clock she'd made a decision she needed to talk to Cat about something, but she knew she needed the conversation to be off duty. Maybe it was perfect that Cat was driving her home that night. She spent the day going over and over in her head what she wanted to talk about.

That evening Raine followed Cat to her car, still debating the logic in talking to her. While Cat was very cool, she was also her boss. What if it crossed some kind of line? Would Cat want her to leave? Raine had no one else to talk to and had to talk to someone.

Cat could tell that Raine was worried about something. But she also knew that asking the girl too many questions tended to send her into hiding. So she waited to see if Raine would bring up whatever was bothering her.

"How's the arm and leg?" Cat asked after a couple of minutes, figuring that was safe.

"Oh, good," Raine said. "San I guess that it was you who gave Natalia my address?"

"She asked if she could go check on you," Cat said, smiling. "What was I supposed to do? I take it she came by?"

58

"Yeah," Raine said, "she got mad at me for not going to the doctor." She looked a little sheepish.

"You didn't go to the hospital after the accident?" Cat asked, surprised too.

Raine shrugged. "I know nothing's broken. It's just road rash and you just basically need to keep it clean."

"Hmmm…" Cat wondered if Quinn and Jericho would agree with that. Both women rode bikes, and had had their fair share of accidents from some of the stories they'd told.

They were both silent for a few minutes as Cat pulled out of the parking garage and headed for the freeway.

"Can I ask you something that isn't work related?" Raine finally blurted out.

Cat smiled, glancing over at the younger woman. "Of course."

Raine bit her lip, still debating the prudence of this conversation, but blowing her breath out, she plunged ahead.

"How can you tell if you're gay?" Raine asked.

Cat raised her eyebrows, staring straight ahead.

"Well I guess that solves that mystery," Cat said grinning.

"Huh?" Raine asked confused.

"Everyone wanted to know if you were gay or not," she said. "I told them I didn't know, that my gaydar was jammed. But it's not, you don't know if you are either," she said winking over at the girl.

"Gaydar?" Raine repeated.

"Yeah, radar for gay people, you've never heard that term before?"

"No," Raine said shaking her head. "Of course I don't have that because I had no idea Natalia was gay until last night."

Cat's head snapped around as she stared at her open mouthed. "And how did you find out?" she asked, her tone slightly raised with her anticipation.

"Well, she mentioned her ex-girlfriend," Raine said, befuddled at Cat's obvious excitement.

"Oh," Cat said, looking crestfallen.

"Did I say something wrong?" Raine asked worriedly.

Cat sighed. "No, I was just daring to hope."

"Hope, ma'am?" Raine asked, thoroughly confused now.

"Never mind, hon," Cat said, waving her hand as if to erase her comment. "You were asking how you can tell if you're gay?"

"Yes."

"Well, are you attracted to women?"

Raine thought about the question for a long minute. "Well, I'm not sure…"

Cat looked at her quizzically. "How do you not know?"

"I look at women and think they're beautiful, or they have a great body or whatever, but I've always thought I was just jealous of them."

"But now you don't think that?"

"Well, since I've been around you and your friends, I see how you all are with each other and your girlfriends, and I think that maybe it's not really that…"

Cat nodded. "Okay, probably a really good person to talk to about this would be Xandy."

"Why?" Raine asked.

"Because she identified as straight until she met Quinn."

"But that was a long time ago, right?"

"Uh, no, about a year, year and a half," Cat clarified.

"Really?" Raine asked, shocked. "They seem like they've been to-gether forever."

"That's 'cause they're a really good match."

Raine nodded in agreement. Quinn and Xandy did seem like the perfect couple.

"So that's one thought," Cat said. "Let me ask you this, are you attracted to men the same way?"

"No," Raine said. "I mean, other than like movie stars and stuff, you know?"

"Yeah, they don't count," Cat said. "Well, what about men you sleep with, does that do the job?" she asked, trying not to put too fine a point on it.

"I've never slept with a man," Raine said.

Cat looked over at her, as she slowed down for traffic. "Have you ever been with a woman?"

"No," Raine said, "that's why I'm not sure."

"You've never had sex?" Cat asked, stunned.

"Nope," Raine said.

"Holy shit!" Cat exclaimed, then gave Raine an apologetic look. "I'm sorry, but you're how old?"

"Twenty-five."

"And a virgin."

"Right," Raine said, not sure what part Cat wasn't understanding.

"You said you grew up in New York."

"Right."

"In the Manhattan area, right?"

"Yes," Raine said, nodding.

"Jesus, I knew Manhattan was an island," Cat muttered. "I just didn't think it was a deserted island…"

"Ma'am?" Raine queried, still completely at a loss as to what Cat was getting at.

"Nothing, sorry," Cat said, shaking her head. "I'm just kind of shocked here Mason, I really am. Okay, well, here's my thinking," she said, "you're probably just gonna have to find someone and jump in and test the water."

"Test the water?" Raine asked.

"Yep," Cat said.

"How?" Raine asked, looking terrified.

Cat couldn't help but laugh at the look on her face.

"Find someone you're attracted to and go for it," Cat said.

"But…" Raine said, looking worried.

"Okay, look," Cat said, "is there anyone you're particularly attracted to at this point?"

"A few…" Raine said, her voice trailing off as she grimaced, looking embarrassed.

"Anyone I know?" Cat asked, grinning. She was sure she already knew it was Natalia.

When Raine didn't answer, Cat looked over at her, the look on Raine's face screamed, *Yes!*

"Oh my God, who?" Cat asked, her eyes wide.

Raine pressed her lips together and shook her head.

"Quinn?" Cat asked.

"No!" Raine said, wide eyed. "I mean, she's nice and all, but…"

"But she's butch."

Raine was lost again. "Butch?"

Cat gave her another shocked look. "You don't know that stuff either?"

Raine shook her head, feeling like she was completely ignorant at this point.

"I never had any lesbian friends," Raine said, shrugging.

"You didn't watch The L Word like half the planet?" Cat asked.

"No cable," Raine said.

"Criminal," Cat said, smiling. "Okay, let's make this easy… There are two main types of lesbian: there are butches and femmes. Femmes use the sink, butches fix the sink; femmes buy the furniture, butches put it together; femmes have their nails done, butches use nails to put up walls and shit…"

"So butches are like the boys," Raine said.

"*Like* boys," Cat said, her tone serious. "But don't get it confused, there are no boys in the lesbian world, and if you call a butch lesbian a man, you'll probably get decked."

"Okay," Raine said, her eyes wide, "so Quinn is butch."

"Right," Cat said, nodding. "So are Jericho and Skyler, although neither of them fit the exact type, but they're more on the butch side than they are on the femme side."

"And Zoey, Xandy, and Jerry are femme," Raine said.

"Right," Cat said, "Devin is too, she's just a bit of a wild child."

"What about you?" Raine asked.

"Ah, me…" Cat said. "According to Quinn, Jericho, and Sky I swing both ways."

"What does that mean?" Raine asked.

"It means I'm both femme and butch. I can be very femme, or I can be very butch. I think it's the cop thing," Cat said. "I don't think too many women can pull off being a cop without being a little bit butch."

Raine nodded, thinking that Cat was probably right about that.

"Okay, so let's get back to what's important here," Cat said. "Who in the group is your type?"

"Well, I think that Zoey is really cute," Raine said, biting her lip.

"Ah, so the femme girls are your thing," Cat said, nodding.

"Well, and you," Raine said, shocking Cat again.

"Uh," Cat stammered, widening her eyes.

"Oh God! I'm sorry," Raine said, shaking her head completely embarrassed. She'd just told her boss she thought she was cute.

Cat chuckled, shaking her head. "It's okay, just don't tell Jovina."

Raine blanched. "I wouldn't do anything…"

64

"Raine, it's okay!" Cat said, laughing. "Really! So, like I was saying you should find yourself someone who's *not* attached, especially not someone who is attached to a very hot tempered Latina," she added with a wink, "and just give it a shot."

Raine looked hesitant, but nodded.

"I really think you should talk to Xandy," Cat said. "I'll send her a text and have her call you, okay?"

Raine took a deep breath. "Okay…"

The very next day, Xandy showed up at the office to talk to Raine.

"You didn't have to come all the way here," Raine told Xandy.

"It's okay," Xandy said. "Quinn had to come down to talk to BJ Sparks anyway, so I thought I'd just stop by."

Raine stood up, looking around, then gestured toward the patio where team members usually smoked. It was empty at the moment.

"So Cat told me what you were asking about." Xandy said out on the patio, smiling at Raine.

Raine blew her breath out, nodding. "She thought you might be able to offer me some insight into what it's like to try to decide if you're gay or not."

Xandy rolled her eyes. "Oh yeah, that was a trial."

"How did you figure it out?" Raine asked.

"Well, I can tell you that I was attracted to Quinn the moment I laid eyes on her," Xandy said. "But I just thought I was infatuated with her because she was so different."

"Different how?"

"Well, she wasn't like anyone I'd ever met before, you know, with all the tattoos and the really butch look that she has…" Xandy's voice trailed off as she grinned. "Oh and the accent, oh my God, so hot…" she said, biting her lip.

Raine nodded, knowing she was seeing someone who was very much in love and almost aching from just seeing it.

"What made you sure?" Raine asked.

"Well, for sure when she kissed me the first time."

"How'd that happen? I mean if you don't mind me asking."

"Well," Xandy said, fondly thinking back at that time. "She'd just come home all scratched up from breaking up with her then-girlfriend and I was trying to clean up the blood streaks…" she smiled. "And our eyes just kind of connected and she kissed me and oh my God the whole world lit up, it was like fireworks going off in my body."

"That exciting, huh?" Raine asked, her eyes practically glowing.

"Oh yeah," Xandy said, "it was followed by a lot of bad stuff, but from that very first kiss, I knew that I was in love with her, and that no matter what, I wanted to be with her."

"You weren't worried about what people would think?" Raine asked.

"I didn't care," Xandy said, "I had found the person I was meant to be with. Once I convinced her of that, I was never letting her go."

Raine sighed, smiling almost sadly. "That's really cool, I just have no idea where to even start."

"Well, I think Cat's right, you need to find someone that you're attracted to and just give it a shot."

66

"That's what she said," Raine said, "but I don't even know how to act or how to approach things with a woman."

"Well, you can ask her to coffee, or dinner…" Xandy said, then gave Raine a narrowed look. "You have someone in mind, don't you?"

Raine bit her lip, but then shook her head. "But it's crazy."

"You don't think my being in love with my butch bodyguard who was dating a movie star wasn't crazy?"

"Maybe to you it seemed crazy," Raine said, "but you're famous and so beautiful, how could she not fall in love with you?"

Xandy blinked a couple of times at the compliment, making Raine realize she'd said that out loud. Suddenly she was red-faced with embarrassment.

"I really didn't mean to say that out loud," Raine said, aghast.

Xandy laughed softly. "It's okay, I do that sometimes too. So who is it?"

Raine shook her head, rolling her eyes.

"Oh my God, it's Natalia isn't it?" Xandy asked.

Raine grimaced, then nodded.

"That's fantastic!" Xandy said, clapping her hands. "You have got to go for it!"

"No, I can't," Raine said, "if there's a league I'm in, she's in the league on the planet farthest from mine."

"Interesting description," Xandy said, grinning, "but I think you underestimate how gorgeous you are."

"Me?" Raine practically squeaked.

"Yes you!" Xandy said, giving her a look that said, *Duh!* "And I think you don't realize that she's already into you."

"No," Raine said, "we're friends, she said so herself."

"Maybe because she doesn't think you're gay, Raine," Xandy said. "You've been jamming everyone's gaydar, I guarantee you that you're jamming hers too."

Raine sighed loudly, looking like she was thinking about the idea, but then she shook her head again. "I just need to set my sights a bit lower," she said, her lips twitching in disappointment.

Xandy frowned, but said no more about it.

After a couple of days of healing, Raine returned to Natalia's class. Cat and the group, who'd discussed Raine's situation at length when she wasn't around, waited to see if she would make a move on Natalia. After a few days it was obvious that was not going to happen, so Cat took it upon herself to pull Natalia aside after class one Saturday morning.

Cat led Natalia off to the side by the office, looking around to ensure that no one would overhear, especially Raine.

"Got a question for ya," Cat said, grinning at Natalia.

"Yes?" Natalia asked, curious about the clandestine nature of Cat's behavior.

"What do you think of Raine?" Cat asked.

Natalia's lips twitched, in reaction to the question. "What do you mean?"

Cat gave Natalia a deadpan look. "Seriously?" she asked. "You know what I mean."

Natalia pressed her lips together. "Why are you asking?"

"Well, it seems that our girl isn't sure about herself," Cat said.

"How do you mean?" Natalia asked, not sure she was grasping the situation. Certainly Cat couldn't mean in terms of the class, because Raine was definitely the best student she had. Natalia hadn't been facetious about that.

Cat sighed, realizing she should have known subtlety wouldn't work on someone like Natalia.

"Look, she isn't sure if she's gay or not, and she needs to try things out. But she doesn't seem to be brave enough to make the approach."

Natalia looked back at Cat, her mouth open slightly in surprise.

"So what are you asking me?" Natalia asked.

"If you were interested in her," Cat said simply.

"Because you want me to *make the approach*," Natalia said, using Cat's words.

"Now you're getting it…" Cat said, grinning. "I mean, if you're not interested, that's okay, but I just thought that you might be."

"Why?" Natalia asked, her eyes narrowed slightly.

Cat grinned at Natalia's suspicion. "Well, I seriously doubt you ask about every student that doesn't show up for your class. Nor do I think you make house calls when they get hurt."

Natalia stared back at Cat, then quirked her lips in a sardonic grin. "I guess I shouldn't let cops into my class," she said, jokingly.

"Not if you want to keep things a secret, no." Cat said.

Natalia nodded agreement. "You are right, I do like her, I just didn't think she was gay."

Cat laughed. "Don't worry, she was jamming all of our gaydar readings too."

"Ah, si," Natalia said, nodding with a wide smile.

"You need to know something, though," Cat said, putting her hand out to touch Natalia's shoulder. "She's completely new to this." She made a circling motion with her hand. "*All* of this."

Raine had just finished showering and was walking out of her bathroom towel drying her hair wearing nothing but a towel when her bedroom door opened. She was surprised when Natalia stepped through the door and looked around. Natalia locked eyes Raine, and turned to walk toward her.

"Hey, what—" Raine started, but Natalia walked right up to her and, taking her face in her hands, kissed Raine's lips.

For a few long moments, Raine couldn't even think past the sensation of Natalia's lips on hers, and the feel of her hands in her still-damp hair. Then as Natalia moaned softly, stepping closer and pressing her body against Raine's, deepening the kiss, Raine regained her senses. She closed the bedroom door and then slid her hands around Natalia's waist gathering her closer still, her hands at the back of the smaller woman's thighs. Natalia pushed upward as she felt Raine's hands supporting her weight, causing Raine to pick her up. Natalia responded by wrapping her legs around Raine's waist, their lips never parting.

Natalia reveled in the feeling of Raine's hands on her legs, and the feel of Raine's hair in her hands. Pulling back she looked down at Raine, whose face was a couple of inches below hers. She took in the sight of Raine with her hair down for the first time. Raine's dark auburn hair, always up in some form or fashion, fell all the way to her waist in tight corkscrew curls.

"Maravilloso," Natalia exclaimed, and she moved to kiss Raine again.

Raine moved to her bed, sitting down on the edge with Natalia's legs still wrapped around her. They kissed for what seemed like forever, things getting more and more heated. Natalia reached up at one point to strip off her tank top, breaking the connection between their lips momentarily. As she moved in again, her lips moved to Raine's neck, her hands smoothing down Raine's arms, pulling at her, her teeth grazing Raine's skin making her shudder. Raine's hands grasped at Natalia's shoulders, she had no idea what to do, but her body wouldn't let her think for long.

Natalia's hands reached between them pulling at the edge of the towel Raine wore, and in moments the sides of the towel fell away. Raine gasped loudly as Natalia's hands moved expertly, making her writhe and finally cry out in an earth-shattering orgasm. She found herself grasping Natalia's back, in an effort to regain her breath. Before she could do that, however, Natalia stood up, kicked off her sandals, and slid off her shorts and exercise bra. To Raine's surprise, she pushed Raine back on the bed, lying over her and within minutes Raine was orgasming again.

Without warning, Natalia lay down on the bed, pulling Raine on top of her as she did.

Suddenly, Raine was completely unsure of what she was doing. She started to shake her head.

"Talia, I don't know how…" she began, not even sure how to say what she meant.

Natalia shifted her body, moving it seductively under Raine's. "Yes you do."

Raine thought about the way that Natalia had moved when she was on top of her, and moved in a way similar to what had excited her so much. Her movements were hesitant at first, but she gained confidence as Natalia moaned, grasping her arms excitedly. Within minutes it was Natalia who orgasmed, her hands pulling Raine's body flush against her, her movements matching Raine's. It was definitely an exciting first experience.

Afterwards, Raine easily lifted Natalia's smaller, leaner frame to position them on the bed more comfortably. Raine lay propped against the pillows at the head of her bed. Her body literally wound around Natalia's, her leg bent possessively around Natalia's waist, her foot flat on the bed. Natalia lay with her upper body angled so she could look up at Raine, and the lower half of her body intertwined with Raine's.

"A dancer's pose," Natalia said, sliding her hand over the leg that crossed her body.

Raine smiled, oddly happy that Natalia recognized the dancer in her.

"You are a dancer, aren't you?" Natalia asked then, her look soft.

"I was," Raine said, her voice quiet.

"Pero no ahora?" Natalia asked, *Why not now?*

Raine looked back into Natalia's eyes, they were so warm and inviting, she felt a pull at her heart.

Finally she shrugged. "Couldn't do it anymore."

"Por que?" Natalia asked why, her voice soft, her look searching.

Raine winced slightly. "Too hard of a story to tell."

Natalia grimaced, sensing the pain that must lie behind that story, so she nodded sympathetically.

"But you were very good, weren't you?" Natalia asked then.

Raine smiled, her eyes soft. "I was okay, yeah."

"Okay, mi ojo," Natalia said, *My eye.* She gave her a sour look. "I know I haven't even seen the tip of that ice cube."

"Berg," Raine said, grinning.

"Ah, si, that's what I meant," Natalia said, her eyes sparkling in amusement.

"Of course it is," Raine said.

They were quiet for a few minutes then, just lying together and absorbing the feelings that seemed to hang in the air along with the music that played from the stereo.

Raine was completely amazed by how comfortable she felt at that moment. She'd never been comfortable in other people's presence, not completely. Not only was she in very close proximity to someone she really didn't know, but they'd just done something incredibly intimate and yet she still couldn't think of anywhere she'd rather be at that moment.

Natalia too was astounded at how good it felt to lie in Raine's arms. For someone who supposedly had no experience, Raine seemed incredibly at ease with this level of intimacy. Natalia had been with lesbians who'd been with many women for many years and were still uncomfortable after sex. Some had to get up and move away, others needed to break the connection quickly, and would only be able to hold stilted conversations which resulted in them both being uncomfortable. Raine, however, seemed completely relaxed and even more settled than she seemed normally.

Smiling at Raine, Natalia canted her head. "What was it you called me?"

Rained looked confused. "What do you mean?"

"Before you made love to me, what did you call me?" Natalia asked, her eyes staring up into Raine's.

The words "before you made love to me" slid right through Raine's heart, making her feel unaccountably happy. It made her smile, and her eyes sparkling as she answered, "Talia."

Natalia bit her lip as she smiled. "I like that."

Raine gave her a sidelong look then. "So should I ask what… or should I say *who* prompted you to come over here today?" she asked, her voice still very comfortable.

Natalia pressed her lips together. "Does it matter?" she asked.

Raine narrowed her eyes, but Natalia read no anger in her look. "I guess it doesn't," she said shaking her head.

"I would have done this sooner," Natalia said, gesturing to their intertwined bodies, "if I'd actually thought you'd be interested."

Raine looked immediately penitent. "I really didn't know myself until you kissed me," she said honestly.

"But when I did?" Natalia asked, her look expectant.

"The whole world lit up," Raine said, smiling.

Natalia knew in that moment that Raine Mason was not only built to be with women, but also built to be probably the most charming soft butch ever known to women.

"Eres peligroso," Natalia said, calling Raine dangerous.

"Why do you say that?' Raine asked, surprised by the word.

Natalia smiled, shaking her head. "So galante y encantador…" she said, her voice trailing off.

"Gallant and charming?" Raine asked, still mystified.

"Si," Natalia said, nodding.

Raine looked doubtful, but shrugged.

"And why do you bind all this beautiful hair?" Natalia asked, running her fingers through it.

"It gets in the way," Raine said with a shrug.

"Then why have it so long?"

Raine grinned. "I had to get it cut a lot when I was a kid," she said. "So when I was able to grow it long, I just let it grow. Now it's really out of control."

"Pero es hermoso," Natalia said, saying that it was so beautiful, lifting a rich red perfect corkscrew curl in wonder.

Raine smiled, shrugging.

Natalia glanced at the clock on Raine's nightstand looking worried for a moment, but then she relaxed.

"What's up?" Raine asked, catching the movement.

"I have class later."

Raine looked confused. "I thought you just had the one on Saturdays."

"No, tonto," Natalia said calling her silly, laughing. "School!"

"Oh," Raine said, looking surprised, "really? That's cool. What are you studying?"

Natalia settled more comfortably in Raine's arms. "Child Psychology."

"Wow," Raine said, surprised, "I thought it would be like fitness or nutrition or something like that." Then she canted her head. "Why child psych?"

Natalia took a deep breath, smiling. "Well, I want to help kids."

"Which kids?"

"Well, any kids," Natalia responded, "but mostly kids that are in the system."

Raine nodded, slowly. "Why them?"

"Well," Natalia said, "when I started out, I really didn't know what type of kids I wanted to help. I knew that I wanted to work with kids, because it's really important, you know?" she asked, giving Raine a questioning look, afraid she was talking too much.

Raine nodded. "Kids are the future of this world," she said, her tone completely understanding.

"Exactamente!" Natalia said, pleased that Raine saw it the way she did. "But then…" she said, her voice trailing off as she realized she was about to talk about something that Raine might not want to hear about.

"But then what?" Raine asked, her voice gentle.

"Well, I met Julie."

"Your ex-girlfriend," Raine said nodding, her voice still easy.

Natalia nodded, her eyes searching Raine's face. She saw absolutely no jealousy there whatsoever. It was a wonderful change from what she was used to with Julie.

"She was in the system," Natalia said, "and it made her a very angry, possessive person."

Raine nodded slowly. "And you thought that if you could fix her…"

"Si," Natalia said, her look embarrassed. "Pero que es una causa perdida," she said, saying that she thought Julie was a lost cause.

"Is that why you two broke up?' Raine asked.

Natalia looked hesitant, her lips twitching in uncertainty. Finally she nodded. "Partly yes."

"Partly?" Raine asked, sounding like a cop for a moment.

Natalia heard it and grinned.

"There were other issues," Natalia said.

Raine looked back at the other woman, knowing there was more to the story, but not wanting to push. Natalia hadn't pushed her on why she'd stopped dancing, and she wasn't going to push on this issue.

Natalia was grateful when Raine didn't ask anymore and felt a rush of gratitude for this woman who seemed so even-tempered. Leaning in, she kissed Raine's neck, inhaling the scent of her skin deeply.

"You always smell so good, but different," she said, somewhat perplexed. "What is that scent?" she asked, recognizing it, but not able to name it.

"Well, right now," Raine said, "it's orange and ginger, because someone kicked my butt in this cardio dance class I take."

Natalia giggled. "Really now?" she said, her look disbelieving. Then she canted her head. "So orange and ginger?" she asked still looking baffled.

"Those scents encourage energy," Raine said.

"And what was the scent when I came here before?" she asked, gesturing to the room.

Raine thought about it. "Well, I was going to bed, so it would have been lavender and vanilla."

"Ah, si, that one I recognize," Natalia said, "good for sleep. But that very first night, when I hugged you after dinner, you smelled maravilloso!"

"You were sniffing me those times too?"

Natalia bit her lip. "You always smell so good."

"Well, that first night my best guess would be that it was eucalyptus and spearmint."

"What does that one do?" Natalia asked.

"It's for stress relief."

Natalia looked back at Raine for a long moment, her look assessing.

"What?" Raine asked, amused by the look Natalia was giving her.

"Aguas profundas," Natalia replied, calling her deep water again.

Later that night, Raine was asleep when Natalia walked into her bedroom. Natalia stood looking down at this woman she was so drawn to, her hair was once again in a long braid. She now wore a loose gray tank top and black shorts. Natalia understood the need for modesty; Raine's roommate had leered at her when he'd let her in a few moments before. Setting aside her backpack, and taking off her shoes, she climbed into the bed.

Raine turned over immediately, smiling as she saw her.

"Hi, I didn't know you were coming back over," she said, sounding pleased.

"Of course I came back over," Natalia said, leaning in to kiss Raine's lips softly.

"Mmm," Raine murmured, reaching out to touch her cheek as their lips met again.

Natalia lay down next to Raine, snuggling close. Raine slid her arm around Natalia's shoulders, holding her close to her side.

"Are you coming to the party tomorrow?" Raine asked.

"What party?" Natalia asked.

"It's like a house warming for some friends of Cat and Jericho. Well, it's really a house viewing, they haven't moved in yet. Either way, do you want to come with me?" Raine asked.

"Are you sure it would be okay?" Natalia asked.

"I'm sure it'll be okay. All the girls will be there."

"How would we get there?"

Raine looked speculative. "Have you ever been on the back of a motorcycle?"

"No, but I'd love to try it," Natalia said, smiling.

"Cool."

Chapter 4

The next morning, Raine woke first. Carefully she got out of bed, not wanting to wake Natalia and went in to take a shower. She did her best to towel dry her hair, and then put it in a braid, knowing that she would be riding later that day, and loose, long hair and motorcycles were not a good combination. Walking back into her bedroom she pulled clothes out of her dresser, glancing over her shoulder at Natalia who was still sleeping. It amazed her that just yesterday, they'd still been instructor and student, and now this beautiful woman was asleep in her bed.

She didn't really dwell on the change of her status, but what did surprise her was realizing she'd never actually imagined losing her virginity to a man. She had thought about what being with a woman would be like, but even then she'd only felt a mild ache for it. What was more important to her, was that she finally felt loved and cared for. She'd begun that journey when she'd met Catalina Roché and when Cat had introduced Raine to her friends, all of whom were gay. The fact that Cat looked out for her, and asked about how she was feeling had begun to make Raine know what it was like to have someone care about what happened to you.

Looking at Natalia, Raine could see a person who might just be someone who would care about her and who she could care for. It had been so long since someone cared about her.

As if she sensed she was being thought about, Natalia stirred. Raine watched as she reached out her hand and touch empty bed. Moving to sit up, Natalia looked around and saw that Raine was standing three feet away with a towel wrapped around her body.

"Didn't we do this yesterday, mija?" Natalia said, grinning.

"You weren't there," Raine said, smiling in response.

Natalia climbed out of bed, moving to stand right in front of Raine, reaching up to wrap her arms around Raine's neck.

"I think I was here," Natalia said, and leaned into kiss Raine's lips. Raine responded by pulling her closer, and Natalia reached between them to remove the towel Raine had on. Within minutes they were making love on the bed, and lay together afterwards. Natalia was snuggled into Raine's side, her face pressed against Raine's neck.

"Eso es todo," Natalia exclaimed, *That is it*!

"What's it?" Raine asked.

Natalia pressed her nose to Raine's neck, inhaling deeply.

"That smell…" Natalia said.

"Eucalyptus and spearmint," Raine supplied.

"Incredible on you," Natalia said.

Raine laughed softly. "If you say so."

"I do."

They lay together for a while, each lost in their own thoughts.

"Raine?" Natalia queried after a few minutes.

"Hmmm?" Raine murmured, pulling her thoughts back to the present.

"Would you mind if we go over to my apartment?" Natalia asked, her tone inexplicably cautious.

"I kind of figured we'd need to," Raine said, her hand caressing the curve of Natalia's waist. "I'm sure you need to change and stuff."

"True," Natalia said, nodding, "but I was wondering if we could spend more time there…" Again there was a look of caution in her eyes.

Raine looked at her for a long moment. "Sure," she said, "but can I ask why you seemed worried when you asked?"

Natalia looked hesitant, but then blew her breath out. She started to say something, but then stopped, her lips twitching in consternation.

"I think…" she began. "Probably it's because of the past…" Her voice trailed off as she shrugged, her eyes not meeting Raine's.

Raine touched her cheek to get her to look at her. "Tell me what that means.

Natalia smiled sadly. Raine was so gentle and open, it worried Natalia that Raine would have to deal with the baggage she carried from past relationships.

Drawing her courage, Natalia looked back at Raine. "Whenever things didn't go as planned, Julie would get angry."

Raine looked back at Natalia, seeing the hurt behind the words.

"Life is messy sometimes," Raine said, her voice practical. "You can't plan everything." She smiled then. "I never planned on you. And yet you are the best thing that's happened in my life for years now."

Natalia stared back at her in amazement, then shook her head slowly as a slow smile started on her face.

"What?" Raine asked.

"Eres fabuloso," Natalia said, telling Raine that she was amazing.

Raine simply shrugged. "I'm just normal."

"Well your normal is pretty amazing." Natalia said, smiling.

Later that morning they pulled up to the front of the Villas of Pasadena. Raine had given Natalia a helmet to wear on the motorcycle. They were planning to leave from Natalia's apartment to go to the party, so they rode the couple of minutes to the apartment. Getting off the bike, Raine looked at the front of the building. It looked nice enough, with double doors into the lobby, and balconies to the side where some of the apartments were.

Natalia led the way to her apartment, and Raine walked along, glancing around at the place. It seemed nice enough, it was very quiet. Outside they walked by the long rectangular pool and barbecue area. It wasn't quite as nice as the one they had at Raine's complex. On the second floor they reached Natalia's apartment. Before she opened the door, Natalia turned around to look up at Raine, her back against the door.

"It's kind of a mess right now," she said with embarrassment. "And I haven't been able to replace the pieces Julie took when she moved out, so it's kind of sparse."

"Okay," Raine said, nodding understandingly.

"Okay," Natalia repeated, as if trying to assure herself that it was okay.

Walking in Raine noticed that the floors were all wood laminate. There was a small kitchen to the left, and a dining area to the right. There was no kitchen table, and there was only a couch, where it was obvious there'd been other furniture previously. There were spots on the walls where pictures or artwork had obviously hung, that were no longer there. There were also boxes sitting in various areas, looking like things were still being packed.

Natalia glanced back at Raine, her look concerned.

Raine caught the look and smiled. "It's nice."

"Not as nice as yours," Natalia said.

"Stop that," Raine said, smiling. "It's just fine."

"It's a good thing you don't really watch TV since I don't have one out here," Natalia said.

"That's okay," Raine said, grinning.

"I have one in the bedroom though, but it's small."

"I'm fine, hon," Raine said, smiling. "Do what you need to do. Just remember you need to wear pants, at least on the ride up there and bring a sturdy jacket."

"Okay," Natalia said, walking into her bedroom.

In the living room, Raine looked around surveying the room. There were a few pictures of people that looked like they might be Natalia's family. There were a couple posters of dance movies. Raine grinned at the Flashdance poster, she loved that movie too. The other poster was from Save the Last Dance, another movie was a favorite.

The apartment itself was fairly small, and it definitely felt like Julie had taken a lot of things with her when she'd left. Raine poked into a couple of the boxes, seeing other pieces of art and electronic equipment. She imagined they were things that Julie hadn't picked up yet. Her lips twitched at what seemed like specifically petty items for Julie to want, but she knew that it was really none of her business. It definitely formed more of an impression of what Julie had been like. Raine was pretty sure she wouldn't like the other woman.

Raine was sitting on the couch when Natalia emerged from her bedroom. She was dressed in jeans, tennis shoes and wore a blouse of greens and blues that hugged her slim figure nicely. She carried a black jacket holding it up for Raine.

"Will this work?" she asked.

"Yep," Raine said, smiling as she stood.

They walked out of the apartment and downstairs to the motorcycle. Raine got on, and Natalia climbed onto the bike behind her.

"Just make sure you hold on" Raine said. "And signal me if you need to stop for any reason, okay?"

"Okay," Natalia said, putting her helmet on and tightening the strap.

The drive to the house in the hills took a little under an hour, traffic was mercifully light because it was Sunday. The hacienda-style house they pulled up to was off on its own road and had a long driveway.

Climbing off the bike, Raine turned to help Natalia off. She reached up to unbuckle her helmet as Natalia did the same.

"Was that okay?" Raine asked her.

"It was great!" Natalia said, her smile bright. Then she turned her head looking up at the house. "Impresionante."

"Yeah, it's pretty awesome looking," Raine agreed.

She noted that Cat's blue Z was there, as well as Skyler's pearlized white Z. Jericho's red Challenger was there, as was Quinn's Mach 1 Mustang. There was also a black Hummer parked on the driveway that Raine didn't recognize.

"Gang's all here," Raine murmured.

Natalia glanced at her, her look searching but she said nothing. Reaching out she took Raine's hand and led her toward the front door.

A beautiful dark-haired woman answered the door. She smiled, and welcomed them into the house.

"I'm Sierra Youngblood-Marshal," the woman said, extending her hand to Raine.

"I'm Raine," Raine responded. "I work for Cat."

"Oh, okay," Sierra said, nodding, then looked at Natalia.

"I'm Natalia," she said, extending her hand to Sierra.

"Oh, I've heard great things about your class," Sierra said, smiling.

"Thank you," Natalia said, smiling back.

"Well, come on in, we're out back," Sierra said, gesturing around the house. "As you can see we have hardly anything in here yet."

It was true. The house was practically empty except for a few pieces of furniture that looked like they were likely new, since they were still covered with plastic. They walked through the house led by Sierra. It was beautiful with rich wood floors and nice accents like archways with painted flowers. There was also a wall-length entertainment center in rich mahogany wood. The kitchen had terracotta tile on the floor and a full wall of brick which held a spot for a fire. It was definitely an amazing house.

Walking behind Sierra, Raine admired the woman's long black hair that flowed down to her waist. It was very obvious she was of American Indian decent with her pronounced cheek bones and almost black eyes; she was beautiful.

As they stepped outside, they saw the beautiful terraced backyard with the pool and barbecue area, as well as the terracotta stone water feature.

The group around the pool looked up seeing Raine standing with her hand in Natalia's.

There were calls of "Woohoo!" and "That's what I'm talkin' about!" and a lot of clapping which had Raine turning ten shades of red, even as Natalia hugged her.

Kashena walked over, and extended her hand to Raine, her smile wide.

"I'm Kashena," she said. "Cat's told me a lot about you. Welcome."

"Thank you," Raine said.

"And you're Natalia?" Kashena asked, having heard about the beautiful dance instructor too.

"Yes," Natalia said, smiling warmly at Kashena.

"What are you drinking?" Kashena asked then. "We've got pretty much everything, beer, wine, soda, liquor… name it."

"Wine, please," Natalia said, "white?"

"Sure, and Raine?"

"Water, please," Raine said.

"Did I just hear water?" Quinn asked, as she walked up.

Raine nodded, her eyes on Quinn.

"No problem," Kashena said, stepping away.

"Leave her alone…" Cat said to Quinn as she walked up, and leaned in to hug Natalia.

"Don't mind the alcoholic," Cat said to Raine, grinning.

Kashena returned with a glass of wine for Natalia and a bottle of water for Raine.

"So you don't drink?" Kashena asked.

"No," Raine said, shaking her head.

Kashena nodded, accepting that answer.

"She just hasn't been a cop long enough," said a blond-haired man who walked up.

"Shut it Baz, not everyone has to drink to cope," Kashena said. Then she looked over at Raine, "Raine, this is Sebastian Bach, he's been my partner for years and he thinks that you have to drink to do the work we all do."

"We do," Sebastian said, shrugging, then he grinned at Raine. "It's good to meet you, you're like ten, right?"

Raine licked her lips, her eyes sparkling with amusement. "A little older than that, but yes, much younger than you."

That had Kashena, Cat, Quinn and Sierra laughing, even as Sebastian nodded. "I like her," he said.

Natalia walked away to go and talk to Zoey and Jericho, leaving Raine standing with Cat as Sebastian and Kashena went over to talk to Sierra about the barbecue.

"So, that looks promising," Cat said, nodding toward Natalia.

Raine glanced over at Cat. "And I guess I have you to thank for that."

Cat quirked a grin. "We take care of our own, Raine," she said. "Better get used to it."

Raine looked over at Cat, her eyes narrowed slightly.

Cat shrugged. "You weren't getting to it, so I got to it for you. If she hadn't been interested, she wouldn't have done anything."

Raine considered what Cat said, nodding then. "I guess you're right. But what do you mean I better get used to it?"

Cat gave her a long assessing look. "It seems to me like you're not used to people looking out for you."

Raine shook her head slowly. "No, not really, I look out for myself okay."

Cat smiled, her look all-knowing. "Well, now you've got other people who are going to look out for you too."

Raine quirked her lips in consideration, then looked back at Cat. "Why?"

"Because we like you," Cat said. "Why is that hard to understand?"

Raine shook her head. "Because most people don't."

"Well, we do," Cat said, "so get used to it."

"Get used to what?" Skyler asked as she walked up to them.

90

"Nothing," Raine said.

"So you and Nat…" Skyler said, holding up her hand, "Nice…"

Raine smiled, high fiving Skyler's hand, looking slightly embarrassed.

"You two make a cute couple," Devin said, walking up and leaning into Skyler.

"Speaking of cute couples," Cat said, "your date is getting close, isn't it?

"Date?" Raine asked, looking over at Skyler and Devin.

"Our wedding," Devin said, her face lighting up with excitement.

"Oh, very cool," Raine said.

"We need to add you two to the guest list," Devin said, elbowing Skyler in the ribs, and Skyler rolled her eyes. "Quit that!" she said, laughing.

"What? Sheesh!" Skyler said, laughing and grabbing Devin around the waist.

Raine really liked the couple, they seemed to balance each other really well. Skyler was the strong quiet type, and Devin was the outgoing one. It was obvious that they were in love too, because she'd often see them just talking and looking each other in the eye. The one thing Raine had seen about love was that if people didn't look at each other when the talked, it meant they weren't really connected.

Later as she looked around the big backyard, Raine could see the couples and the way they connected. Jericho and Zoey were standing talking to Natalia. Jericho's arm held Zoey close to her side, Zoey's hand was touching Jericho's waist and stomach as they talked. Kashena and Sierra stood arm and arm, talking to Sebastian, Skyler and Devin by the barbecue. Cat and Jovina stood near the pool, talking and holding hands.

Walking over to where Natalia stood, Raine wasn't sure what to do, but Natalia solved that for her, by holding out her hand. Raine took it and Natalia pulled her in, wrapping Raine's arm around her waist, so she could lean back against her. Raine found that she liked the feeling of Natalia leaning on her. She slid her other arm around Natalia's waist, kissing the side of her head.

"You can't say that it's not right, if you don't understand the purpose," Jericho was saying.

"Then what is the purpose?" Natalia was asking.

"It's a sign of modesty," Jericho said. "But it's also a sign of religious faith."

"But why do they have to cover their faces?" Natalia asked.

"Because to their way of thinking, only her husband should see her face, or her hair; it's something that should be saved for him."

"But don't you think that's just men forcing women to do what they want?" Natalia argued.

"Believe or not, some women really prefer it," Jericho said.

"Historically, women have been forced to wear the hijab and niqab, but Middle Eastern society is changing and it's not always an issue anymore," Zoey put in.

"But you, obviously don't do it," Natalia said, looking at Jericho.

"No, but I've never been a practicing Muslim. My father is though," Jericho replied.

"Does your mom wear that stuff?" Natalia asked.

"No, but she respects my father's religion and his beliefs," Jericho said.

Natalia glanced back at Raine. "What do you think of all that?"

Raine looked at Jericho, and then at Zoey. "I think women should be able to do whatever they believe in, no matter what."

Jericho grinned and inclined her head. "Well said."

"What's going on over here?" Cat asked as she and Jovina strolled up.

"We're talking about middle eastern culture and where women fit into it," Jovina replied.

"That's a dangerous topic," Sebastian said as he walked up to the group.

"For the one man here," Kashena put in as she and Sierra joined them.

"I can hold my own," Sebastian said confidently.

"That's what we've heard," Sierra murmured.

"Oh-ho!" Sebastian said, giving Sierra a narrowed look.

"Maybe we should talk about women's treatment in the military," Kashena said.

"Yeah, that sounds like a good topic," Skyler said, as she and Devin walked over.

No one noticed when Raine eased back from the group , to go and look at the water feature. Natalia watched as Raine stood with her back to the group, shifting her weight from one foot to another. After a few minutes, Natalia eased away from the group too and went to join her.

Moving to stand behind her, Natalia slid her hands around Raine's waist, resting her cheek against Raine's back.

"Estas bien?" she asked, wanting to know if Raine was okay.

Raine reached down to cover Natalia's hands with her own.

"Si, estoy bien," she answered, *Yes I'm okay.*

Moving to stand in front of Raine, Natalia looked up at her.

"What's wrong?" she asked.

"Nothing's wrong," Raine said, smiling softly, "I just get really restless in big groups."

"Why?" Natalia asked.

Raine shrugged. "Don't know, it just gets overwhelming."

Natalia nodded, reaching up to touch Raine's cheek.

Cat watched the two from where she was stood with the group, smiling. It seemed like a really good match and she was happy to see it.

"What are you doing?" Jovina asked her, seeing her watching the other couple.

"They look happy," Cat said.

Jovina looked over at them too. "Yes, they do. Maybe they're both what the other needs."

Cat looked down at Jovina. "You mean like us?" she said.

Jovina smiled. "Yes, like us."

Later, the food was ready and everybody gathered to eat. Raine received a lot of grief for only eating a small amount of food and most of it being the fresh vegetables that were served.

"Don't tell me you're a vegetarian…" Sebastian said. "I was just starting to like you…"

"I'm not a vegetarian old man," Raine said. "This," she said holding up a piece of chicken, "is chicken which, last time I checked belongs in the meat section."

There was a round of "ohs" that had Sebastian grinning.

"I simply eat clean," Raine said.

"Clean?" Sebastian repeated.

"They teach you that at Juilliard?" Cat asked, grinning.

Raine narrowed her eyes at her boss, but nodded.

That had Natalia staring at her openmouthed. "Juilliard?" she queried.

Cat canted her head at Raine. "You still haven't told her that?"

"We've been together less than forty-eight hours," Raine said, rolling her eyes.

"Told me what?" Natalia asked, her grin evident.

Raine looked at her, and then shook her head. "Maybe I should try beer…"

"Here ya go," Sebastian said happily, handing Raine his beer.

Raine took a drink and immediately made a face, which had everyone laughing.

"Here, try this," Quinn said, handing her a Guinness.

"Oh God, don't drink that!" Cat said.

Raine tried the Guinness and grimaced. "It's not as bad as that one," she said, gesturing to the Heineken that Sebastian drank.

"Okay, try this," Cat said, handing her a Shock Top Belgian white.

Raine tasted that and nodded. "Oh much better."

"Excuse me!" Natalia exclaimed, her hands on her hips. "If you all could stop trying to get my girlfriend drunk…"

"Ohhhhh…" Jericho said, grinning.

"You tell em!" Xandy said, laughing.

"Juilliard?" Natalia asked, looking at Raine.

Raine rolled her eyes and sighed. "I have a Bachelor of Fine Arts from Juilliard, okay?"

Natalia blinked a couple of times. "That's the Juilliard in New York, right?"

"Yes," Raine said, nodding.

"And?" Cat said, her eyes sparkling.

"And what?" Raine replied, giving Cat a narrowed look.

"And what other degree do you have?" Cat said, not letting up.

"You have two degrees?" Natalia asked, her look shocked.

Raine shrugged. "The second one is easier to get," she said.

"Aye dios mio!" Natalia said. "Tienes que estar bromeando…" she muttered, saying, *You have got to be kidding me*, which no one else understood.

Raine grinned. "Lo siento. Estás realmente enojado?" she said, saying she was sorry and asking if she was really mad.

She managed to shock everyone around them with her accent that sounded quite like Natalia's.

"No, I'm jealous!" Natalia said. "And I knew you could speak it perfectly," she said, narrowing her eyes.

"Solo un poco," Raine said, grinning as she said 'only a little'.

"Bullshit," Natalia said succinctly.

Everyone laughed at that. It was a fun afternoon.

Raine drove them home, stopping at Natalia's apartment to let her out. She didn't see the disappointed look that crossed Natalia's features as she removed her helmet. She then leaned forward and kissed Natalia's lips.

"I'll call you tomorrow?" Raine asked.

Natalia nodded, giving a slight smile. Raine put her helmet back on and rode off. Natalia watched her ride away, her lips twitching, then she sighed and walked to her apartment. She was hoping Raine would have stayed with her.

A few hours later, Raine was lying in bed, trying to go to sleep. It was ten o'clock by that time and she needed to be up at five the next morning for work. Sleep was illusive for her quite often, but on this night it just seemed worse. Finally, she used the remote for the Bose and turned on some music, hoping that would distract her enough so she could sleep. Unfortunately, still sleep wouldn't come. She sat up rolling her neck, trying to push away the visions of the dark-haired beauty who'd been with her in that very bed that morning. Nothing was working.

She was just about to get up when her bedroom door opened. Natalia stood in the doorway, looking cautious. Raine smiled immediately.

"Hey…" Raine said, smiling brightly. "I was just thinking about you."

"You were?" Natalia asked as she stepped inside the door and closed it behind her.

Raine nodded, as she moved to put her feet on the floor, still sitting on her bed. Natalia walked over to her, stepping between Raine's legs, and putting her arms around Raine's neck.

"I missed you," Raine said, staring into Natalia's eyes.

Natalia bit her lip, smiling as she did. "Then why did you leave?"

Raine looked surprised by the question, then she shrugged. "I didn't know how this kind of thing is supposed to go," she answered honestly.

Natalia smiled, leaning in to kiss Raine's lips softly. She pulled back to look into her eyes. "What did you think?"

"That we'd spent so much time together you might be tired of me at this point," Raine said.

Natalia smiled, shaking her head. "You obviously haven't heard the joke about lesbians and U-Hauls."

"Huh?" Raine queried.

"Never mind," Natalia said, moving to kiss Raine again, wrapping her arms tighter around her neck and pressing closer.

They kissed until Raine moved her hands to the backs of Natalia's thighs, lifting her so Natalia's legs wrapped around her waist. Then she moved back on the bed, moving to lean against the headboard, still kissing Natalia. They made love, each of them reaching their climax together. Afterwards, Natalia lay against Raine, her head on Raine's shoulder; both of them were still clothed, articles of clothing had simply been shifted during their lovemaking.

Raine had her arms wrapped around Natalia, and she lay with her eyes closed, enjoying the feeling of Natalia being close against her.

"You know, "I never really thought about being with a man..." she said, sounding a bit puzzled on the last.

Natalia lifted her head. "So you always knew you were gay?" she asked.

"No," Raine said, shaking her head, "I didn't. I just thought women were beautiful, or sexy, but I never realized it was because I was interested in them."

Natalia looked back at her. "That makes sense. Are your parents anti-gay? Because that could explain it too..." Her voice trailed off at the odd look that crossed Raine's face. "What?" she asked then.

"I really don't know if my parents are anti-gay," Raine said, her tone odd.

"What do you mean? How could you not know? Did it never come up?" Natalia asked.

Raine bit her lip, her look reticent.

"Raine?" Natalia queried, not sure what was happening.

Raine took a deep breath, and blowing out she said, "I never met my father. And my mother left me at a park when I was five."

"What?" Natalia said, shocked. She searched Raine's face for signs that she was kidding. "You were in the system?" she asked when she realized Raine was definitely serious.

Raine nodded. "For ten years."

"And you didn't tell me," Natalia said, sounding hurt. "Even when I told you about Julie…"

Raine looked contrite, but shrugged. "I just don't really talk about it."

"Like Juilliard?" Natalia asked.

Raine didn't answer, she just looked back at Natalia, her eyes showed her discomfort.

"Wait, you said ten years," Natalia said. "What about the other three?" she asked, knowing that kids aged out of the foster system at the age of eighteen.

Raine shifted, her shoulder twitching slightly in a half shrug. "I never showed up at the home they tried to shift me to when I was fifteen. I kind of got myself lost."

"Lost?" Natalia asked.

"I kept going to school," Raine said, "so no one seemed to notice."

"But where did you live? Where did you stay?" Natalia asked, horrified at what she was hearing.

"Wherever," she said simply.

"Wherever?" Natalia repeated, disbelieving.

Raine nodded, blinking a couple of times.

"But how did you get into Juilliard?" Natalia asked.

"One of the homes I was in was trying to impress social services so they put me in a ballet class. I liked it, so when they quit paying, I made a deal with the teacher to clean up and stuff so I could keep taking her class."

"How old were you?" Natalia asked.

"Like nine," Raine said, sounding very young at that moment.

"So how did you end up at Juilliard?"

"They had open auditions, anyone could try out. So I did."

"And they accepted you," Natalia said.

"Yep," Raine said.

"How did you pay for it? I imagine Juilliard isn't cheap."

"Scholarship," Raine said.

Natalia stared back at her for a full minute, her mind trying to assimilate what she was hearing. She'd decided that Raine must have come from parents with money in order to have gone to a school as prestigious as Juilliard. Now she was finding out that not only did Raine not come from a stable family, but she had obviously struggled to get where she had.

"You must be really good for them to have given you a scholarship," Natalia said.

Raine shrugged again. "I guess."

"You guess?" Natalia repeated, the beginnings of a smile on her face.

Raine said nothing, just looked back at Natalia. She wasn't sure if this was the end of the questions, but they were coming close to a very uncomfortable subject, so she was hoping it was.

"So I guess that blows my theory out of the water," Natalia said.

"Theory?" Raine asked, surprised by the change in topic, but relieved by it as well.

"That Julie is messed up because of the system," Natalia said.

Raine looked back at her for a long moment and then said, "Julie's messed up because that's how Julie is made."

Natalia looked at Raine. "And you're not, because you're not made that way."

"Right," Raine said, nodding.

"Will you tell me more about your experiences some time?" Natalia asked, having sensed Raine's tension around the topic, but happy that she'd at least told her.

Raine nodded, her look solemn.

Natalia leaned in kissing Raine's lips. "Thank you for telling me," she said softly.

Then she put her head against Raine's chest, her hand reaching up to touch a tendril of long curly hair that had come loose from Raine's braid. Natalia realized the impact of what Raine had just told her. This woman had been through so much, and yet she'd come out the other end, strong and still a sweet person. How was that possible?

Two weeks later the group gathered at Kashena and Sierra's house once again, this time to help them move in. There was a moving truck and loads of boxes. Everyone also had the opportunity to meet Colby, their thirteen-year-old son. They found that he was polite and very respectful. Everyone loved him instantly. With his light hair and dark eyes like his mother's, he was definitely a heart breaker.

Sebastian was also there helping with the heavier stuff. Sierra, ever the organizer, had all the boxes labeled and all the rooms labeled with corresponding numbers. It wasn't long before half the truck had been unloaded and Kashena called an official break.

Kashena, Sebastian, Skyler, Jericho and Quinn all stood on the back patio smoking while the rest of the group put together lunch. Colby was tasked with taking beers out to the group outside. He did so with pride.

"He's a sweetie," Cat commented to Sierra.

Sierra smiled. "Yes, fortunately nothing like his father, and a lot like Kashena."

"What happened to his father?" Natalia asked "If you don't mind my asking."

"No, it's okay," Sierra said, "his father is in prison in Sacramento."

"Oh," Natalia said, shocked.

Sierra grinned at the girl's reaction. "He did it to himself," she said. "First he hit me in front of Kashena, then he made the mistake of trying to attack her."

"He hit you?" Devin asked in disbelief.

"Yes," Sierra said, "I was leaving him and he wasn't happy about it."

"Had he hit you before?" Zoey asked.

"No," Sierra said. "But he had been different since he'd come back from Iraq," she said, her look far away.

"He was in Iraq?" Devin asked, glancing out the window at Skyler.

"Yes, he was a Marine, like Kashena was," Sierra said.

"Oh, I didn't realize Kashena had been a Marine," Devin said. "Was Sebastian one also?"

Sierra smiled, remembering the time Kashena had told her about her and Sebastian's first meeting.

"No, Sebastian was an Army Ranger," Sierra said. "They fought each other the first time they met."

"Like knock down drag out?" Xandy asked, looking shocked.

"Yep," Sierra said, smiling as she looked out the window at Kashena. "It ended in a draw and they became best friends over a bottle of Jack Daniel's."

Devin chuckled. "That sounds about right," she said.

There was a ring of the doorbell at that moment, Sierra looked perplexed. "Uh, okay… not expecting anyone else," she said, then went to answer the door.

Sierra opened the front door and beamed. "Oh my God!" she exclaimed.

"I thought you could use some extra hands," said Midnight Chevalier.

Standing behind her was her husband Rick Debenshire, Joe Sinclair, John Machievelli, Randy Sinclair, as well as Kana and Palani and their four-month-old baby.

"Is that my girl?" Sierra said, cooing at the baby. "Come in. Come in!"

The group walked in, greeting Sierra with hugs and friendly comments.

Raine stood staring in awe as the Attorney General for the State of California walked in.

"You've never met, Midnight, have you?" Cat asked, grinning.

Raine shook her head, her mouth still hanging open.

Cat laughed, and took Raine's hand to lead her over to Midnight who was hugging Zoey.

"Midnight," Cat said, touching Midnight on the shoulder. "This is Raine Mason, she's a member of my team at LA IMPACT."

Raine suddenly had a pair of gold-green eyes trained on her, and she was fairly certain she was going to die.

Midnight grinned, having gotten used to the way people acted around her. Putting out her hand, she touch Raine on the hand. "Hi," she said, smiling.

"Hello, ma'am," Raine said, her tone very official.

"Call me Midnight," Midnight said, her smile warm.

"I... oh..." Raine stammered, "I don't think I can..." she said, her tone awed.

Midnight laughed. "Sure you can, I even got Zoey to stop calling me ma'am," she said, winking at Zoey.

"She doesn't work for you, ma'am," Raine replied immediately.

"Jesus, are you scarin' people again?" Rick said, his sapphire-blue eyes twinkling as he walked up, hugging Cat. "How are ya, love?" he asked Cat.

"I'm good, Rick. You remember Jovina?"

"I do," Rick said, smiling at Jovina, leaning over to kiss her on the cheek. Then he looked over at Raine and Midnight. "Give it up, Night, these kids are trained in the academy to call you ma'am, gonna have to deal for a bit."

Midnight sighed, reaching out to touch Raine on the hand again. "Just know you're allowed if you choose to, okay?"

Raine nodded numbly.

Midnight grinned, and shook her head, then she moved to greet the others in the room, before walking outside.

"You alright?" Cat asked Raine.

"They're legends…" Raine said.

Cat chuckled. "And you didn't even grow up in California."

"I heard of her in New York," Raine said. "She's like famous all over the country. So is her husband, and is that Joe Sinclair?"

"Steady," Cat said, grinning.

"Hey Cat," Joe said, walking up and hugging Catalina. His light blue eyes then moved to Raine not recognizing her. "Hi, I'm Joe," he said, smiling and extending his hand to Raine.

Raine nodded to him, barely remembering to put her hand out. Joe grinned.

"And you are?" he asked.

"I'm Raine, Deputy Raine Mason, sir."

"I'm retired love, you can't call me sir anymore," Joe said, winking.

"Yes, but," Raine stammered.

"No, buts. It's Joe or hey you," he said, grinning.

Again, Raine nodded, not willing to call him either at that point.

Outside the comments were flying, and the group was laughing uproariously by the time Sierra told them that food was ready.

"Are you okay?" Natalia asked Raine, who still looked a bit dazed.

"Talia, you have no idea who those people are…" Raine said.

"Sure I do," Natalia said.

"Okay, but they're like rock stars in the law enforcement community."

Natalia smiled, she found it extremely endearing that Raine was so awed by these people. She knew that Midnight was the Attorney General and that Rick Debenshire, her husband, was well known, as was Joe Sinclair. She didn't know a lot about them, but she knew enough to understand Raine's discomfort.

During lunch there was a lot of fawning over Kana and Palani's baby, Anone Akua Sorbinno. The little girl was a beautiful dark-haired baby doll. There was also a lot of good-natured ribbing about the $1.7 million mansion they were all sitting in at that time.

"The State is paying you entirely too well, here," Devin said, grinning.

"Excuse me, Miss *I don't get out of bed for less than a hundred thousand…*" Skyler said, mockingly.

"Yeah, how much did that house in Malibu cost, doll?" Quinn asked, grinning.

"Bite me!" Devin said, grinning.

"Tell me when and where," Quinn said, winking.

"Don't make me kill you here in front of all these cops," Skyler said to Quinn.

"I can do it for you," Xandy said, narrowing her lavender-blue eyes at her girlfriend.

"Only kidding love, don't get yer knickers in a twist," Quinn said to her girlfriend and winking at Skyler.

"Army pilots are mean..." Sebastian said, grinning.

"Hooah," Skyler intoned.

"Hooah," Sebastian replied.

"Ah crap, I'm out numbered," Kashena said.

"Nope, Navy Seal here, close enough, right?" John Machiavelli said, grinning.

"Oo rah," Kashena said, grinning.

"Any port in a storm, huh Marine?" Sebastian said, raising an eyebrow.

"Die Ranger, just die," Kashena said, shaking her head.

"All in good time," Sebastian said.

"Okay, you two," Sierra said, giving her wife a nudge.

"Uh-oh, wife alert," Sebastian said.

"Don't make me come over there," Sierra said, narrowing her dark eyes at Sebastian.

Kashena started to laugh, as Sebastian held his hands up in surrender.

Later, they all got back to unpacking the truck, but by sundown everyone was exhausted. Everyone had been invited to stay at the house; some stayed, others left. Natalia insisted that they stay, since she didn't feel that it was safe for Raine to ride back down the hill, as tired as she was. They ended up in a spare bedroom. It was obvious to Natalia that Raine was exhausted, but she didn't seem to be able to settle down to sleep.

"What can I do?" Natalia asked, watching Raine pace like a caged panther.

Raine looked over at her; Natalia was sitting in the middle of the bed, her hair pulled back from her face with a clip. She was wearing a hot-pink tank top with the word "work" printed on it in black and a pair of black bikini underwear. Raine still couldn't believe how beautiful this woman was and that she was lucky enough to be dating her.

"Nothing, hon," she told Natalia. "I just can't seem to relax right now."

"Ven aqui," Natalia said, patting the bed.

Raine looked back at her, her look cautious. "Why?"

"Just come here!" Natalia exclaimed, laughing as she did.

Raine walked over to the bed and climbed up on it. Natalia reached out taking Raine's face in her hands, pulling her close so she could kiss her lips.

"Now, lie down, on your stomach," Natalia ordered. "Wait. Take this off first," she said, gesturing to the tank top that Raine was wearing for bed.

Raine sighed heavily, then complied. Natalia moved to straddle her waist and began massaging Raine's back, starting from her lower back and working her way up slowly. Raine moaned softly, feeling muscles that had been overworked that day tightening, then slowly loosening up under Natalia's touch.

When Raine was completely relaxed, Natalia leaned down; she kissed Raine's shoulder, then her shoulder blade, then her other shoulder and that shoulder blade, moving lower and lower kissing every inch of skin. By the time she got to Raine's lower back, Raine was turning over and pulling Natalia down to her, kissing her lips deeply. They made love then as quietly as possible and lay together afterwards, Raine falling asleep feeling relaxed and completely content.

"So how are you feeling about the house?" Sierra asked Kashena in their bedroom that night.

Kashena quirked a grin. "I'm still adjusting," she said.

"I know," Sierra said. "It's a lot of house."

"Yeah, it is," Kashena said. "Do you still like it?" she asked then.

"More now, actually," Sierra said, smiling.

"Well, then we're here," Kashena said, grinning.

"It was really nice for Midnight to come by," Sierra said.

"It was nice of her to come by with help," Kashena said.

"Well, that too," Sierra said. "Oh, we have to make sure we get Colby registered for school this week," she said. "Their school year starts in August here."

"Yikes, that's the week after next."

"I know!" Sierra said, nodding. "That's why I'm saying we can't forget."

Kashena sighed, there was a lot to do in a short amount of time. The beginning of the week she was reporting to her new unit. She'd heard a lot about the unit she was taking over and she wasn't looking forward to dealing with some of the personalities she'd heard about. There were some definite bad apples in the barrel and she needed to weed them out and get some better quality people assigned. Kashena would be running the Covert Operations and Informant Development group. She'd already been informed that the unit was running amok; they hadn't had a leader in some time. One member had already decided he was going to be the leader when Kashena was put in charge. Kashena knew she was going to have a problem with that particular member.

Sierra's challenge was to get the Los Angeles AG's office up and running on the newest electronic case management system. All the other offices were utilizing the system but her Deputy Attorney General III, a supervisor, in the Criminal Division in Los Angeles had made a series of excuses as to why her office wasn't using it. Midnight had finally gotten fed up when one too many cases had slipped through the cracks, causing delays in capital trials, making Midnight's office look bad. She'd assigned Sierra to take charge of her people in that division and wanted her to work with the other Deputy AGs to get everyone on track. Sierra knew Midnight was counting on her, and she had no intention of letting her boss down.

Chapter 5

A few days after the move at Kashena and Sierra's house, Raine needed to put her bike back in the shop. She had been experiencing problems with it not getting enough fuel and sputtering, so she had talked to Quinn and Jericho, who both rode motorcycles, and they had suggested she take it in when they couldn't find anything wrong with it. Cat had offered to pick her up for work, but Natalia had said that Raine could use her vehicle.

Natalia followed Raine to the repair shop, wincing and worrying every time another vehicle got even close to Raine. She found that she was a lot more nervous about seeing Raine ride than she was when she was on the bike with her. She also realized that she was very attracted to Raine on that motorcycle with her black leather riding jacket with its sapphire-blue accents. She'd taken to wearing leather chaps over her jeans since her last accident. Leather chaps would have prevented the road rash she'd received on her leg. Natalia found everything about her sexy, especially on that motorcycle!

Once they'd dropped off the motorcycle, Natalia handed Raine the keys to her car.

"Uh," Raine stammered looking confused.

"You're dropping me off at school, so it's easier if you're driving," Natalia said.

"Oh, okay," Raine said, moving to open the passenger door for Natalia.

Raine got in on the driver's side, and had to adjust the seat, since Natalia was about four inches shorter than she was. She adjusted all the mirrors then finally started the car.

"This is weird," Raine commented, as she put the car in gear to leave the bike shop.

"What is?" Natalia asked.

"Driving a car again," Raine said, grinning as she pulled out onto the road.

"How long has it been?" Natalia asked.

"Uh," Raine stammered, having to think about it. "I'd say about seven or eight years."

"Wow!" Natalia exclaimed. "Why so long?"

"Well, in New York having a car is a luxury I really couldn't afford. I learned how to drive one, but I never owned a car. A motorcycle is easier and cheaper to have in New York. My first bike cost me three hundred bucks."

"Mierda!" Natalia exclaimed. "That's cheap!"

"Insurance is cheap, so is gas, and you can park 'em pretty much anywhere," Raine said.

"I see," Natalia said, nodding, understanding more why Raine road a motorcycle. "But you can probably afford the insurance and gas now, right?"

"Sure," Raine said. "But why bother? I own the Shadow outright, and I can spend money on other things."

Natalia shook her head. "I still owe money on this."

"This is a lot more than my Shadow, that's why," Raine said, grinning.

Before long they were at the college. Raine pulled up to the curb and put the car into park.

She turned to Natalia. "Text me your last class place and time, so I make sure I'll get back here on time," she said.

"Okay," Natalia said. She leaned across the console to take Raine's face in her hands and kissed her lips softly. Then she kissed her a second time but deeper.

"You're making it hard to go to work now," Raine murmured against her lips.

Natalia laughed, enjoying that Raine was willing to tell her how much she wanted her. Julie always played the uninterested game. It had made Natalia seriously wonder if she was less attractive to her. It hadn't been a good situation at all. Raine was so very different and she loved that.

"I will see you later," Natalia said, smiling brightly.

"Go learn lots," Raine said, winking at her.

"Voy a!" Natalia replied, as she got out, *I will!*

Raine watched her until she disappeared around a corner, then she put the car back into gear and headed to work. Her day was busy, filled with writing reports and a warrant for Cat to sign. So it seemed like only a couple of hours before she looked up and noted that she needed to get ready to go pick up Natalia. The body shop had called and it was going to be a while before they could get to the Shadow, so she needed to look into a rental car or something.

At the college, she found a parking spot, and using the information Natalia had sent earlier, she looked for the room where Natalia's last class was. She was walking quickly because she was running a couple of minutes late and didn't want to miss Natalia. As she walked up however, she saw that she hadn't missed her at all. She'd been delayed, by a woman who had to be Julie.

Raine saw the way they were talking, and it looked heated. She hung back to give Natalia a little privacy, although it didn't seem that Julie cared about that. Looking at Julie, Raine saw how really butch the woman was. She was about two inches shorter than Raine, but very different in body style and overall appearance. Raine could see what people meant by the difference between a butch lesbian and a soft butch lesbian. Julie was stocky with cropped dirty blond hair, almost military style, and she had a few prominent tattoos, one of which was a large skull and cross bone on her neck. She wore baggy jeans with combat style boots, and a button down gray shirt. She looked very hard.

As Raine watched, Julie took a menacing step toward Natalia, and when Natalia shrunk away, Julie grabbed her arm roughly. Raine then strode over to the two women, stepping up beside Julie.

"Let her go, now," Raine said, her voice strong but low.

Julie glanced at her, made a dismissive sound, and turned her attention back to Natalia.

"Last time I'm gonna tell ya," Raine said, her tone stronger now, taking on the cop authority as she stepped closer to Julie.

Julie let go of Natalia in surprise that this soft butch was pushing up on her. She wheeled around to face Raine, pushing her chest out, her chin coming up.

"Who the fuck do you think you are?" Julie sneered.

Raine's eyes didn't even flicker at the tone in Julie's voice. "I'm the one that told you to let her go. I'm also the one that's telling you that if you lay hands on her again, you'll deal with me."

Julie looked back at Raine, her face a mask of disgust. She turned slightly, like she was going to walk away, but then threw a punch. Raine was ready for it; she brought her arm up blocking the punch and used her other forearm to shove Julie back away from her.

Julie looked shocked. She'd been sure that this woman was no threat to her. Raine's blue eyes remained completely passive.

"Are we clear now?" Raine asked, as she held her hand out to Natalia who was staring at her wide-eyed.

Not waiting for Julie's answer, Raine nodded to her, still cool and calm. Then with Natalia's hand in hers, she turned and walked away with Natalia beside her. Neither of them spoke until they reached the car. Raine opened the passenger door for Natalia, taking a long look around, then got in on the other side.

Turning in the driver's seat she took Natalia's hand in hers.

"Are you okay?" she asked.

Natalia nodded, then looked at her with wide eyes. "How did you do that?"

"Do what?" Raine asked.

"Deal with her so easily," Natalia said, her voice indicating her awe.

Raine looked back at Natalia for a long moment. "Babe, you know I deal with much worse people than her on a daily basis, right?"

Natalia looked back at her for a long moment a little shocked, then she shook her head. "No, I guess I never really did think about that. I mean, I know you're a police officer, but you never really seem like one… Does that make sense?"

Raine grinned, inclining her head. "I don't usually bring the job home with me," she said. Then her face turned serious. "That's not the first time she's grabbed you like that, is it?"

Natalia blinked a couple of times, wanting to lie, because the truth was so embarrassing, but she couldn't lie to Raine. Finally she just nodded her head.

"I didn't think so," Raine said, her look pained. "Is that one of the other reasons you two broke up?"

"Yes," Natalia whispered.

"You know that what she was doing and what she just did now is not okay, right?" Raine asked. "No one should ever lay hands on a woman like that, ever."

Natalia drew in a breath, and blew it out as she nodded. "I know,"

"But she had her reasons and her excuses…" Raine said.

"Which now, thanks to you, I know are complete bullshit," Natalia said.

"Glad I could help," Raine said, grinning.

Natalia smiled at her in return.

"She's got to get the idea that coming at you like that is not going to be allowed," Raine said then.

"I know, and the girls tried to help," Natalia said.

"The girls?"

117

"You know, Cat, Jericho, Quinn, all them," Natalia said. "They were at the gym when Julie was there one time and basically threatened her." She shrugged. "Julie just started coming here instead."

Raine's lips twitched in irritation. "Pretty hardheaded, I take it."

"Oh yes," Natalia said.

"Well, then, that changes what I was going to talk to you about," Raine said, grinning.

"Okay," Natalia said, her tone unsure.

"My bike is going to need to be at the shop for at least a week. I was going to rent a car, but if you don't mind, I think I'd like to become your chauffer for a bit."

"Okay…" Natalia said, her look a little perplexed.

"How often does Julie show up?" Raine asked.

"Every other day or so," Natalia said, then she caught what Raine was thinking. "Oh, honey, I don't want you to have to deal with her…"

"Talia, I'm not going to stand by and let her hurt you," Raine said, her look puzzled. "You didn't think I would, did you?"

Natalia didn't answer, she just looked down at her hands in her lap. Raine reached over touching Natalia's hands, looking at her until she raised her eyes again.

"I'm not going to let her hurt you," Raine told her. "If nothing else, it's my job to protect you, but as your girlfriend, I need to protect you, okay?"

"I didn't want to drag you into any of this…" Natalia said.

"You should have told me about this sooner," Raine said, her tone chastising.

Natalia didn't answer, just bit her lip.

Raine looked at her for a long moment, then leaned in to kiss her lips softly. She drove them back to Natalia's apartment then. They had time to eat a quick light dinner and then needed to get to Natalia's dance class.

During the class Natalia noted, to her dismay, that suddenly the gay members, the ones that Julie had always considered her "groupies" were suddenly paying far too much attention to Raine. Raine didn't even notice. She never paid attention to women or men flirting with her. It happened a lot when she was on patrol, usually people trying to get out of tickets. By the middle of class, Natalia was ready to chew nails. The women were purposely playing with Raine, running their hand down her arm when they talked to her and making a lot of eye contact. Natalia constantly had to scream at them to pay attention, to get them refocused on the class and less focused on Raine.

When they took a water break, Natalia walked over to Raine.

"Lo que esta mal con ellos?" she asked Raine, wanting to know what was wrong with "them."

Raine looked confused. "Who?" she asked.

"Estás bromeando?" Natalia snapped, asking if Raine was kidding.

Raine's eyes widened at the tone in Natalia's voice. "No…" she said, shaking her head.

Natalia shot her a look of complete disgust, but then turned to start the class again. After that, anytime Natalia's eyes connected with Raine's, Natalia could see that Raine was trying to read her look. Was it possible that Raine hadn't noticed? How could she not notice?

After the class was over, Raine stood waiting for Natalia to get her gear together, and Natalia could see that Raine was still mulling over what had happened. When Natalia gestured that they could go, Raine pushed off the wall, walked over to take Natalia's gear bag out of her hand, and leaned in to kiss her softly on the lips, the same as she would any other night.

Some of the girls from Raine's group, Cat, Jovina and Jerry, were still out in front of the gym when they came out.

"Everything okay?" Cat asked. She'd noticed Natalia's tension and the girls flirting with Raine during class and Raine's complete oblivion at the situation.

Raine nodded, and Natalia glanced up at her.

"Did you not notice?" Natalia asked.

"Notice what…?" Raine asked, her look cautious.

"Wait, what did you notice?" Natalia asked, sensing that she and Raine were not talking about the same thing.

"Okay, let's move this outside," Cat said. She could see that people were watching the exchange closely, and thought this was not something that should be said inside the gym.

Cat led them outside, Jovina and Jerry stayed back, sensing that Cat was there to referee the argument they felt brewing.

Natalia turned to Raine, looking up at her. "So what did you notice?" she asked, her hands on her hips.

Raine looked back at her for a long moment, her look almost amused by Natalia's stance, which served to only further irritate Natalia. She saw Natalia's eyes narrow and had to stifle the laugh that threatened to come out.

"What I noticed was you estar loca tonight," Raine said, her tone completely devoid of any kind of accusation.

"Me?" Natalia said, her voice raised.

Raine rolled her eyes and nodded.

Natalia launched in a series of expletives all in Spanish, which had Raine looking at her like she was insane.

"Okay, okay," Cat said stepping between them, before Natalia launched an all-out offensive against Raine, who very obviously had no idea what this was about.

"Raine," Cat said, looking at the other woman. "What has Natalia sputtering over there is that those girls in the class, who were paying so much attention to you tonight, were flirting with you."

"Huh?" Raine said, looking genuinely confused.

"They were flirting with you mija!" Natalia exclaimed.

"What, why?" Raine asked.

"Aye dios mio!" Natalia exclaimed, throwing up her hands.

Raine looked at Cat. "They are interested in Talia, not me, why would they flirt with me?"

Cat looked over at Natalia. "She has a point."

"Que? De que estas hablando?" Natalia said.

"Babe, she has no idea what you just said," Raine said.

"I got some of it," Cat said, grinning.

"What are you talking about?" Natalia asked, trying not to grin at Raine's input.

"They were probably flirting with her to piss you off," Cat said.

Natalia stared back at Cat openmouthed. Then she looked over at Raine, who simply looked back at her calmly.

"And I did exactly what they wanted…" Natalia said.

"Yep, you got mad at your girl, instead of them," Cat said.

Natalia looked flabbergasted, then she looked over at Raine again and put her arms around Raine's waist, leaning her head against her chest.

"Lo ciento, carina," Natalia said quietly, telling Raine that she was sorry.

"It's okay, babe," Raine said, looking over at Cat and mouthing the words "thank you" to her boss.

Cat smiled and nodded and left them alone to go back inside and retrieve Jovina.

The next night in class, Natalia waited until everyone was there, seeing that the girls were right back to their game. This time she got everyone's attention on her, then she turned and walked straight over to Raine, put her hands up to cup Raine's face, and pulled her head down to kiss her deeply. Raine's hands slid around her waist and pulled her close, deepening the kiss. Everyone in class catcalled and cheered, except for the three who'd been flirting with Raine. They did not look happy.

Cat sauntered over to the three girls.

"Might wanna take note of that, ladies. That's what you call good sex," she said with a wink.

It was the third day that Raine had driven Natalia to school, and she was back to pick her up. For the second day in a row, she had made the point of turning her badge face forward. She also used her hip holster instead of the one she usually wore at the small of her back. That day both were effectively covered by the black button up shirt she was wearing over a black tank top, the cover shirt was held together with one button at her waist. She also wore jeans and black boots.

As she walked into the quad outside of Natalia's class she glanced around, not seeing Julie. Looking at her watch she saw that she was about fifteen minutes early. She moved to lean against a wall close to the class, but out of the way of where people would be exiting.

Ten minutes later, Julie walked up from another direction. She didn't notice Raine since another class had let out just then, and the sidewalk was filled with people. Raine, however, spotted Julie and moved toward the door to Natalia's class.

Julie spotted her, her look was openly hostile. Raine looked back at Julie, completely calm. She stood with her feet braced apart, her arms in front of her, hands clasped together in what was essentially a parade rest for police officers. Julie was at a disadvantage because when the door to the class opened, she was behind it and Raine quickly took a step forward, her height allowing her to spot Natalia before she got to the door. As Natalia reached the door, Raine took her hand and pulled her away, before Julie even had a chance to touch her.

Natalia knew something was wrong the minute she saw Raine's face; she was looking to the right, and she was tense. That's when she saw Julie. The three of them stood looking at each other while everyone moved around them, and the area cleared.

"Did you need something?" Raine asked Julie, her tone conversational.

"I need to talk to Natalia," Julie said, stepping toward Raine, her look aggressive.

"Go right ahead," Raine responded, putting her arm around Natalia's shoulders. It was her way of saying, *While I'm standing right here.*

"Could you give us some privacy?" Julie glowered.

"Not gonna happen," Raine said, her voice even, her eyes staring directly into Julie's.

Julie took a couple of steps toward Raine, who immediately stepped around to completely block her from Natalia, her lips curling in derision.

"I don't think you want to do that," Raine told Julie.

"I think you don't know what I want to do!" Julie said, flexing her arms, her hands balled into fists.

"Let me repeat," Raine said. She unbuttoned the single button of her shirt and swept the sides back to reveal her badge and gun. "I don't think you want to do that."

Julie's eyes went to the gun first, then to the gold star that identified Raine as a Deputy Sherriff for the County of Los Angeles. Raine noted that Julie's eyes widened when she read the badge, then her eyes went to Raine's.

Julie glowered in impotent rage. The thought, *The bitch is a cop!* rang in her head.

Raine reached back, taking Natalia's hand. Giving Julie one more pointed look to make sure the message had been received, she turned and walked away with Natalia close at her heels.

In the car, Natalia looked over at Raine.

"Que era muy caliente…" Natalia said, waving her hand like she was fanning herself, telling Raine *that was really hot.*

"You think so, huh?" Raine asked, grinning.

"I really like the butch cop thing," Natalia said, smiling.

Raine gave her a sidelong glance as she started the car. "Butch cop thing?" she repeated.

"Mmmhmm," Natalia murmured, grinning. She reached over and slid her arm around Raine's, hugging her arm close.

Raine just shook her head.

When they got back to Natalia's apartment, Raine was changing to get ready for Natalia's class, and was just taking her gun out of its holster, when Natalia walked into the room. Raine didn't notice.

"Wait!" Natalia said, walking over to where Raine stood by the dresser.

"What are you doing there?" Natalia asked, pointing at the gun in Raine's left hand that was pointed at the floor.

"Securing my weapon…" Raine said, her voice trailing off thinking that was a given. Then she realized that she'd never done this in front of Natalia before.

"So," she said, her voice taking on an instructional tone, "I'm removing the ammunition clip." She showed Natalia where the release button was for the clip, slid the piece out of the weapon and laid it aside on the dresser.

"There's still a round in the chamber, and since you're not familiar with guns, I'm going to take it out too. So to do that, you have to pull back on the slide," she said as she did so, "and then drop the round out like so."

"What happens to that bullet?" Natalia asked.

"It goes back into the clip," Raine said, picking up the clip and levering the bullet into the magazine top.

Raine then set the gun down next to the clip.

"So, now it's secure?" Natalia said, her voice stumbling over the unfamiliar word.

"Yes, now it's secure."

"Okay," Natalia said, smiling.

Raine didn't explain that she had a backup weapon in her gym bag, and that she was basically always carrying a weapon in one form or another. This had been enough for one night.

***

Kashena stared back at the man that had been acting as the lead for her unit before she'd been assigned.

"I'm sorry," she said, her look disbelieving. "Did you say you haven't been tracking the officers' hours?"

"No," Greg Fulham said, shrugging, "they keep that shit in their diaries."

Kashena pressed her lips together, doing everything she could not to roll her eyes, blowing her pent up breath out slowly in an effort to calm herself.

"You were signing their timesheets though, right?" she asked then.

"Yeah," Greg said, not for the first time in this conversation looking at her like she was nuts for asking.

"Were you looking at the diaries when you did that?" Kashena asked then.

"No," Greg said, looking mystified as to why he'd do that.

"So you took their word for it, that they were giving you the right hours?" Kashena asked briskly.

"They're cops," Greg said, as if Kashena herself wasn't a cop, and that cops could always been trusted.

Kashena canted her head at the man, unable to even think of a response that wouldn't get her written up by the SAC. She'd gotten the distinct impression that the Special Agent in Charge of the Los Angeles Interagency Metropolitan Police Apprehension Crime Task Force, known as LA IMPACT, wasn't much more connected than the man she was dealing with at the moment.

"Ever heard the term, 'any case worth working is worth working on overtime'?" she asked him.

"Yeah, that one's good," Greg said, nodding with a grin.

Kashena looked back at him, her face very serious.

"Okay," she said, her tone reflecting her exasperation, "I think we're done here." She stood to signal the end of the meeting and gestured to the door so he could leave.

Sitting back down in her chair, Kashena thought to herself, *Left a good job in the city...* as she sighed mightily. This was not the first extremely frustrating meeting she'd had with Greg Fulham, and she was sure it wouldn't be the last. She fully intended to send him back to the agency from whence he came as soon as she could. In fact she was planning to return more than half of the eight people that worked for the unit. There were three people who seemed to know what they were doing; the rest seemed to be there for the easy paycheck.

The program's numbers were in the basement and Jericho wanted something done about them. Kashena knew she couldn't do it with the current team members. She knew she needed to document the problems and the shortcomings in order to send the officers back to their departments. She also planned to review applications to the unit and do a thorough background check on the people that were asking to come join LA IMPACT. If they weren't stellar where they were, or have something to bring to the table, she didn't want them in her unit.

It was something she discussed with Sierra at length that night as they lay in bed.

"I know exactly what you mean!" Sierra said, after hearing Kashena's recap of her day and her meeting with Greg Fulham. "Half of the people in the division here are just as reluctant to use the automated system as the manager that was blocking the whole thing. It's crazy!"

"I'm not sure if we should kiss Midnight, or kick her in the ass," Kashena said, grinning.

"Maybe a little of both?" Sierra said, grinning.

Two days later, Kashena finally got her group out on a raid to round up some local violent offenders on parole. The raid targeted individuals who were on parole and were suspected of having weapons in their homes or on their person. Unfortunately many parolees weren't anxious to go back to prison, and as such were happy to do whatever it took to get away. With Kashena's ill-trained and out of practice team, it was left to her to run down one of the suspects and tangle with him. It resulted in a few nasty bruises; a couple of which were hard to hide from her wife.

Kashena was just getting out of the shower when Sierra came in. They'd driven separately that day, since Kashena had no idea how long her raids would go. She'd hoped to be dressed before Sierra got home, though the bruise on her neck would be impossible to hide for long.

"Oh my God!" Sierra gasped at the dark bruise on Kashena's back. "What happened?'

Kashena turned around and saw Sierra's eyes go directly to her neck, and then down to her upper thigh.

"Wait, wait, wait," Kashena said, holding up her hands to forestall the firestorm she could see brewing in her wife's eyes. "It was a raid, and parolee's don't like prison…"

"Where was your backup?!" Sierra growled, her eyes narrowing. "Baz would never have let any of that happen to you…"

Kashena tilted her head. Sierra was right about that, Sebastian always had her back.

"I know, babe," she said, her tone calm in an effort to calm her wife. "But these guys and girls aren't Baz, and it's what I've got to work with right now."

"No," Sierra said, shaking her head sharply. "That's not acceptable." Then she pointed at Kashena. "Do any of them look like this tonight?" she asked sharply.

Kashena winced not only at the question, but at the pointed tone of her wife's voice. Stepping over to Sierra, Kashena touched her cheek, her blue eyes searching Sierra's dark eyes.

"I know, babe," she said to Sierra. "I know this is hard... and you've never been with me when I was actually doing the cop thing..."

"The cop thing?" Sierra repeated her tone still sharp. "Is that code for getting the crap beat out of you?"

Kashena grinned, which only caused her wife's eyes to narrow more. "Okay, okay, I know, it looks bad, but babe, this is kind of standard for raids sometimes. You get bumped, you get bruised. Bad guys really don't like to be taken down, and some of them are stupid enough to fight back." She touched Sierra gently under the chin. "This is the job sometimes."

Sierra crossed her arms in front of her chest, her look all lawyer at that moment. "Well, I'm not really fond of the job right now."

Kashena had to press her lips together to keep from smiling at Sierra's tone. Sierra saw it and even though she maintained a straight face, her eyes danced in amusement.

"But you still love me..." Kashena said.

"Sometimes," Sierra said, turning her head away like a spoilt child, as Kashena moved to pulled her closer.

"You love me..." Kashena said, her tone cajoling.

"Maybe," Sierra said, keeping her face turned away.

"You know you love me…" Kashena said, leaning down to move her lips over Sierra's exposed neck.

"Stop that…" Sierra said, already sounding weak.

"Are you sure…" Kashena said, sliding her arms around her wife, her lips moving up to her ear. "Are you really sure you want me to stop?" she whispered in her ear,, her hands sliding up Sierra's back.

"Well, maybe not…" Sierra said, sighing.

Kashena's lips claimed hers then and they were done talking for a while. There were a few times when Sierra would touch one of the bruises and Kashena would jump, which would get Sierra wanting to complain again, but Kashena would quickly get her attention again.

Afterwards, they lay together, and Sierra gently touched the bruise on Kashena's neck.

"I really don't like this," she said, her voice soft.

"I know, honey," Kashena said, "I'm sorry, but you married a cop."

"You weren't this kind of cop when I married you," Sierra said.

Kashena looked back at her for a long moment. "If I'd been this kind of cop then, would you still have wanted me?" she asked calmly.

"I've always wanted you, Kash," Sierra said. "I think this would have scared me more then, though."

"Why?" Kashena asked.

"It's just so much more violent," Sierra said, shaking her head.

"Sweetheart, you were married to a Marine," Kashena said. "You didn't think that was violent?"

"Kash, it was violent, over *there*," Sierra said, and Kashena knew she meant in the Middle East where her ex-husband Jason had been stationed.

Kashena nodded. It explained why when Jason got violent with her the first time, she'd come running to Kashena. She stared back at Sierra for a long time, not sure what she could say.

"Babe, I don't know what I can say here," Kashena finally said, honestly.

Sierra shook her head. "I don't expect you to say anything, Kashena, I love you, it's just an adjustment I need to make."

Kashena stared back at this woman she loved more than life itself, and for the very first time since they'd gotten married, she saw a chink in their armor. It was not a comfortable feeling and she fell asleep that night with a cold hard knot in her stomach.

Two days later, in her office, Kashena was reading over a report and making corrections on her computer when the visions ripped through her head.

"Son of a…" she muttered, as she braced her hands on her desk as the pictures flashed in her head. The images were rather appalling and she had to sit taking slow deep breaths until her vision cleared, and then the headache hit. That was right when Sebastian walked in to pick her up for lunch.

"Uh-oh," he said, seeing her face, "Vision?"

Kashena shook her head, closing her eyes.

"What did you see?" he asked, pulling out his notepad.

"Two bloody eagles, a knife blade and…"

"And?" Sebastian queried.

Kashena looked back at him, her face somber. "The Ojibwa symbol for death."

Sebastian felt his heart stop for a moment, and he moved to sit down in the chair closest to him. He stared at Kashena openmouthed for a full minute. Then he closed his mouth, shaking his head.

"No, that's not what it means," he said, still shaking his head.

He knew what she thought it meant, that she was going to die, he would not accept that, not her.

Kashena looked back at him with a pained expression, knowing that what she'd just told him had hurt him to his core. She wanted it to be wrong, she really did.

Not now... she thought, sending the message to her ancestors, *I'm not ready...* but she knew her visions told the story and that she couldn't change them even if she didn't like what she saw.

* * *

Almost a week after her encounter with Julie, Raine found herself in a fairly violent altercation. She'd gone to a bike shop after work one evening, wanting to do some tuning on her bike, but needing a few things. When she'd left the shop someone had been leaning on the wall near her bike.

As she stepped closer she saw that what looked like a man, was actually a very butch woman. The woman was taller than Raine by a good four inches, and at least twice Raine's body width; none of it looked like fat.

Raine took stock quickly. There was about five feet between them. Her gun was locked in her saddle back, but she had a snub-nose revolver in an ankle holster. Her badge was in her pocket, but she was fairly certain from the way the woman was looking at her, that she already knew she was a cop and didn't care. That wasn't a good thing.

"You need something?" Raine asked, her tone calm as she chewed the gum in her mouth.

"Yeah, I'm Jake. You're fucking with one of my friends," the woman said, "and I don't like it."

"We all have things we don't like," Raine said simply.

"Yeah, well, I'm gonna do somethin' about that," the woman said, pushing off the wall suddenly and striding toward Raine.

Raine stood her ground, the last thing she was going to do was let this woman think she was intimidated by her. She lifted her chin slightly, her body tensing. Jake came in swinging. Raine dodged the first punch, but got caught by an uppercut, that had her head snapping back. She staggered backwards, but didn't go down, and surprised Jake, by stepping into the next punch, dodging it as it went past her face. She grabbed that arm and using the momentum Jake already had behind the punch, flipped the bigger woman over her shoulder. Jake landed with a thud, but scrambled to her feet quickly. Raine had just enough time to side step a kick that would have taken her legs out from under. Fortunately being a dancer meant that she was able leap high enough to avoid the kick, and manage a spin kick that caught an unsuspecting Jake in the face. She was down for the count.

Reaching up to touch the blood on her lip, she knew she wasn't going to be making an appearance at Natalia's class tonight. Putting a booted foot on Jake's motionless body, she reached down and pulled out her revolver, and then pulled out her phone. She called the sheriff's office and had them send out a car.

By the time she filled out the report and got Jake booked for assaulting a peace officer, she was exhausted. She ended up texting Natalia mid-way through telling her that something came up and that she'd see her later, since she had no idea how long it would take to get done at the station.

As it turned out, she got to Natalia's apartment two hours after Natalia had already gotten home. She knocked on the door, and she could feel her face aching a bit. She'd taken a lot of ribbing at the jail for the bruise on her mouth, until the other officer had brought Jake in and then the guys in the jail were nodding their heads. It amused her no end that they assumed because she wasn't the classic tough looking body shape that she couldn't handle herself.

Natalia opened her door ready to be angry about Raine being so late, but then she saw the bruise. Immediately she put her hand to Raine's face, her look aghast.

"Raine what happened?" she exclaimed, her dark eyes scanning Raine for any more bruises.

"It's just the one," Raine said, grinning. "Can we go inside please?" she asked as she glanced at a guy coming down the hallway and feeling rather personally exposed.

"Of course," Natalia said, moving back so Raine could come inside the apartment.

"What happened?" Natalia asked immediately.

Raine set aside her backpack, and moved to sit on the counter of Natalia's kitchen. Natalia moved to stand between her legs, looking up at her.

"I met one of Julie's friends," Raine said.

"Aye dios mio!" Natalia bit out angrily. "One of Julie's friends did this?"

"Easy now…" Raine said, grinning, seeing the hot Latina temper getting ready to explode.

"Who was it?" Natalia asked, obviously still seething.

"Uh, Jake?" Raine said.

"Estás bromeando?" Natalia asked, shocked, wanting to know if Raine was kidding.

"I kid you not," Raine said, her tone serious.

"Jesucristo…" Natalia muttered, shaking her head, then she looked up at Raine. "You were able to use your gun, right?"

A grin tugged at Raine's lips. "Why do you ask it that way?"

"Ella es enorme, pasado, mala culo!" Natalia exclaimed, saying that Jake was huge, hulking and a bad ass.

"Well, regardless of all that," Raine said, trying not to be hurt by the fact that Natalia didn't actually think she could have handled Jake without the use of her weapon. "No, my weapon never cleared leather, and Jake is now resting in jail."

"Never cleared leather?" Natalia repeated, her voice stumbling over the unfamiliar phrase. "Que significa esta?" Natalia asked, wanting to know what that meant.

"It means," Raine said, her tone wry, "that I held my own against your ex-girlfriend's giant of a friend."

"Never cleared leather," Natalia repeated, knowing she hadn't just heard the explanation of that phrase.

Raine brought her knee up, putting her foot on the counter, lifted her pants leg and pulled her backup weapon out of its holster slowly.

"This," she said, as she pulled the weapon out, "is clearing leather." She then put the gun back into the holster and again slowly pulled it out.

"So pulling it out of that," Natalia said, pointing to the holster.

"Yes, pulling it out of the leather holster," Raine said. "Clearing leather."

"Aw," Natalia said, understanding. She shook her head. "Cops use weird phrases," she muttered.

"Y los Mexicanos no lo hacen?" Raine said, *And Mexican's don't?*

"Exacto," Natalia said with a grin.

"Uh-huh," Raine murmured, grinning too.

Natalia moved closer, reaching up to pull Raine's face down to hers so she could kiss her. Pulling back she looked up into Raine's eyes.

"I'm sorry that this happened," she said, her finger gently touching the bruise. Then she shook her head, slowly. "Maybe this is too much," she said, sounding forlorn suddenly.

"Too much?" Raine repeated her look inquisitive. "What's too much?"

"This," Natalia said, her hand circling between them. "You're getting hurt, attacked, it's peligroso, no bueno," she said, her look pained.

Raine looked back at her for a long moment. "So you're saying that we shouldn't be together because Julie can't control her jealousy?" she asked, her tone calm.

"You're getting hurt…" Natalia said.

Raine suppressed the smile that wanted to bloom because of Natalia's concern. Once again Raine realized how good it felt to have someone worry about her. It was all the more reason to stay, not to go.

"Do you think I don't get hurt doing my job, normally?" Rain asked, her tone soft.

"Yes, but that's work, not us."

"You don't think our relationship is worth more to me than my job is?" Raine asked then.

Natalia stared back at her, unable to answer that question.

Raine hopped off the counter, taking Natalia's face into her hands, to tilt her face up to hers.

"I love you," Raine told her, "and you're worth everything to me."

She was rewarded with the most brilliant, beautiful smile she'd ever seen. Natalia reached up putting her hands around Raine's wrists.

"You mean that?" Natalia asked, obviously a little afraid to believe it.

"I don't say things I don't mean, Natalia," Raine told her.

Natalia nodded. "I love you too," she said, "Tanto." *So much.*

They kissed then, and ended up making love in the kitchen and then moved to the bedroom where they made love again. Lying together afterwards, Natalia's fingers brushed the multiple earrings in Raine's left ear.

"Why so many?" she asked. It was something she'd been curious about for a while.

Raine grinned. "One for each foster home I was in," she said simply.

"That many?" Natalia asked, counting the earrings. She counted a total of eleven.

Raine nodded. "At least one a year and one year, two of them."

Natalia blew her breath out, shaking her head. "How did you grow up to be this wonderful person that you are?"

Raine shrugged. "Who I was built to be, I guess," she said.

"No," Natalia said, "you're a whole other thing, Raine."

"What does that mean?" Raine asked, looking perplexed.

"It means that you got through something like that with so little lasting damage, it's amazing."

"Oh, there was damage, believe me," Raine said, her look serious.

Natalia looked back at her. "Can you tell me?" she asked gently.

Raine settled more comfortably on the bed. "Well, I don't remember much about the first few homes. I have impressions of fighting, and yelling and feeling like I wanted to hide all the time, which I did. It's what got me kicked out of the third home I was in. The woman said I was too difficult to keep track of, which was code for, *she's never around when I want to her to clean something…*"

As Raine talked, her hand on Natalia's waist moved in what Natalia assumed was agitation, and she was pretty sure Raine didn't even know she was doing it. She just listened, her look a mixture of pain and sympathy.

"When I was about ten, one of the foster family's teenage sons tried to rape me, so I kicked him in the balls. That got me kicked out of that home," Raine said, her tone even.

"They didn't do anything about him attacking you?" Natalia asked aghast.

"Nope," Raine said. "It was actually somehow made out to be my fault, can't remember how they got there with it, but… By this time I was taking the ballet class and I'd met my best friend."

Natalia looked confused, she'd never heard of a best friend before. "Who?"

"Her name was Aurelia, I called her Auri, because the rest was just too long," Raine said, with enough sadness that Natalia sensed that this was a source of pain for her.

Natalia nodded, wanting Raine to continue and not wanting to interrupt with too many questions, even though they were filling her mind.

"She made things a little better," Raine said. "And she was the one that suggested I get an ear piercing for every home. I think she thought it might somehow influence my getting something permanent." Again the sadness was there, in her eyes, and in her voice.

"Was she good at ballet too?" Natalia couldn't help but ask.

"Oh yeah," Raine said, smiling. "She liked to say that she was born with ballet shoes on."

Natalia smiled at that. "Is she the reason you auditioned for Juilliard?"

Raine looked back at her, then nodded slowly. Natalia could sense that she was tensing and the last thing she wanted was for her to close up, so she asked a different question.

"So what happened after that last home, with the boy?" she asked.

Raine blew her breath out, looking thoughtful. "I think that was the time I got the hippie couple," she said, grinning. "They were the ones that taught me about 'eating clean.' They actually encouraged my ballet thing."

"What happened with that home?" Natalia asked.

Raine pursed her lips, her look sardonic. "The man was a bit too 'free love' with the neighbor lady and his wife caught him, so they were divorcing and had to give up fostering."

Natalia laughed at the description, but shook her head sadly. "So the one good home you found and it didn't last."

"Kind of par for my course," Raine said, shrugging. "A few more homes, and the last one was the one that finally made me decide that I was done being fodder for their mill."

"What happened there?" Natalia asked, almost afraid to hear.

Raine closed her eyes slowly, then opened them again. "They were a Mexican family, with three kids of their own plus two other younger fosters. I became their full time babysitter. The minute I got home from school it was my job to do everything, cook, clean, take care of the baby…" Natalia waited, knowing that what was going to come wasn't good.

"The baby got sick," Raine said, "and I told them that the baby was sick. They wouldn't do anything; they wouldn't take him to the hospital, they wouldn't call a doctor… Finally when I was sure that there was no other way, I went to the emergency room with him. I told them the baby was mine, and I told them what had been happening with him. It turned out he had pneumonia and they needed to keep him for a few days. My foster parents flipped, because now they had to go get him and pay the doctor's bills and explain why I brought him in and they didn't, when I was only fifteen. They were in hot water, and they blamed me for it. The baby ended up dying, and they blamed me for that too."

"Oh Raine…" Natalia said, reaching out to touch her cheek, tears in her eyes. "You know it wasn't your fault, right?"

Raine nodded, not looking like she really believed that, but not saying so. "After that I just did my own thing."

"And ended up at Juilliard," Natalia said.

"Yeah," Raine said.

"With Auri," Natalia said softly.

Raine simply nodded, her look somber.

"What happened?" Natalia asked, her tone both soft and cautious.

Raine took a slow deep breath, blowing it out just as slowly, visibly gathering the courage to talk about the subject. The look on her face showed desolation.

"Auri was the best friend I'd ever had," she said, her tone haunted. She smiled sadly, her eyes looking down at Natalia for a few moments. "She was a lot like you, actually," she said, tears gathering in her eyes. She looked away again, as if she needed to distance herself from what she was saying. "She was the one that tried to take care of me, brought me sandwiches from her parents' house when we had class because she'd never know if I'd eaten or not, try to give me her allowance money because she knew I needed it for the train or the bus, always stuff like that..." Her voice trailed off as she stopped to regain her composure, swallowing convulsively against the tears that tried to come again and again.

"I honestly think she was the first woman I was in love with, but I didn't understand it at the time," she said, shrugging. "Anyway, we got through Juilliard together, and believe me that wasn't easy. She pushed me, I pushed her, we helped each other study, we helped each other practice... And we got through it..." she said, her voice trailing off again as she fought back more tears. "And then we graduated and wonder of wonders we both made the dance company and decided to cut loose in the city. We bar hopped, got stupid drunk," she said, grinning wistfully, "and then we ended up at this local club, one in Spanish Harlem. I'd gone to the bathroom, because I was really messed up and I was hoping I could throw up and feel less drunk. I heard a loud noise outside the bathroom and I heard people screaming and running. I came out of the bathroom and tried to find Auri. At first I couldn't find her. I started hearing that there'd been a drive by and that people had been shot out front. So I went outside..."

Natalia closed her eyes, knowing what was coming, but not wanting to be right.

"She'd gone outside to talk to some guy," Raine said, smiling sadly. The tears came sliding silently down her cheeks as she said the rest. "She'd been hit twice. She bled to death in my arms."

"Oh God..." Natalia said, reaching up to pull Raine to her, crying as hard as Raine.

They lay quietly for a long time. Raine's hand was on Natalia's shoulder, her thumb moved back and forth, her look still haunted.

"After that, I couldn't dance," she said. "I lost my spot in the company. They said they understood and that I could come back, but… I was done with dancing then."

Natalia nodded, now understanding why Raine would graduate from a place like Juilliard but not become a professional dancer. It was too wrapped up in her friend, the woman she'd loved.

"How did you come to be here?" Natalia asked.

"Picked the place on the map that was furthest from New York," Raine said. "Fell into the law enforcement thing." She shrugged. "I guess I wanted things like drive-bys to stop happening."

Natalia just shook her head. All of these things had happened to this woman, and still she was caring and sweet. Julie hadn't been through half of what Raine had. It was a sobering thought.

Chapter 6

Things between Kashena and Sierra were still tense. Kashena was doing her best to cope with the stress, but it didn't help that her team seemed to completely unable to do their jobs without assistance. In the week following the first raid, things just got worse. Kashena got to see first-hand how inept Greg Fulham really was. He'd applied for a warrant, and gotten a judge to sign off on it. Ten minutes before the raid, someone had been looking the warrant over and found that Greg had put the wrong case number on it. They'd had to cancel the raid, which had included an aviation wing as well as another enforcement unit from another division. Kashena had had it with him.

She'd just gotten off a call with Jericho, telling her why her team had just completely blown a raid and wasted numerous staff hours. The SAC didn't like Kashena because she made it obvious to everyone that more could be done if you actually *worked* at it. It was making everyone look bad, so the SAC had taken his first opportunity to slam SAS Marshal for her team's 'screw up.' Kashena had been called by Jericho who had not blamed her in the least, and had said that they should get together to talk.

Kashena was standing outside, to the side of the agency building, smoking her third cigar since getting out there. She was leaning against the wall, one booted foot up on the wall behind her. Where she stood was an alleyway between two buildings, so she was surprised when a man walked up from the back area of the building.

He was a tall, bald, black man; he looked about thirty-five and very fit. In her head, Kashena thought, *Marine*. She nodded to him, expecting him to walk past her. Instead he stopped and asked her for a cigarette. Reaching into her pocket she pulled out her pack, showing him.

"Sorry, this is all I have," she said.

At that moment, a cop car went by on the street, and it caught Kashena's eye. As she turned her head to look at it, she heard movement behind her. She turned just in time to see a gun being pointed right at her head.

"This is for Jason," the man said simply as he pulled the trigger.

Moving with split second reflexes, Kashena swung her left arm around to slam into the man's arm, simultaneously drawing her own weapon from its holster and bringing it up as his gun fired. She felt the impact hit her, but was focused on shooting him to eliminate the threat. She hit him square in the chest and he went down instantly with a very surprised look on his face.

"Fuck!" she screamed, blowing her breath out, and starting to pace as people started to come out of the building having heard the gunshots. "Fuck, fuck, fuck," she chanted, still pacing, then stopping as the pain hit her Doubling over, she realized she'd been hit in the side.

"Marshal!" yelled one of the men from her team as he came running toward her

"Get Bach on the phone, now..." Kashena said, her voice strained from the pain she was in.

"Ma'am, we need to get an ambulance..." the man started to say as he pulled out his phone.

"Get Bach first!" Kashena growled, as she swallowed against the desire to throw up. Her legs were shaking, and someone helped her to sit down, leaning against the building.

She jumped as someone else pressed something to the bleeding wound.

"Sorry," said the person. Kashena realized it was Raine. Raine was already on the phone with the EMTs telling them they had an officer down.

"Did you get him yet?" Kashena asked.

"Yeah, here," the guy said, handing her the phone.

"Baz," Kashena said, gasping at the end of it as a wave of dizziness hit her.

"What's going on?" Sebastian asked, his tone sharp.

"Get to Sierra and Colby, now, get to them now Baz…" Kashena said, her voice fading as she blacked out.

Sierra was in her office when Sebastian walked in unannounced, which was completely unlike him so it told her something was wrong. She stood from her desk immediately.

"We gotta go," Sebastian said, holding his hand out to her.

Sierra began to move immediately. "Is it Kash?"

Sebastian nodded. "I'm sending an officer for Colby."

As she took his hand and let him lead her out of her office, Sierra felt terror sweep over her. What wasn't he telling her? They got downstairs and out of the building. He put her in his Hummer and got in on the driver's side. He started the vehicle with a roar, and threw it into gear.

As he screeched around another corner, Sierra looked over at Kashena's best friend. His eyes were stormy, his jaw set tight.

"Please tell me what's happening." Sierra said, her voice the barest whisper.

Sebastian glanced over at her, "I'm not sure," he told her. "But she told me to get to you, and now I've heard that she's been shot and they're taking her to Beverly Hospital. So I'm getting you there as fast as I can."

Sierra closed her eyes, trying not to think about what would happen if Kashena was gone. This was the sum of all her fears coming to fruition; she felt as if she'd brought it upon Kashena herself.

In the driver's seat Sebastian was doing his best not to lose it altogether. Was this it? What she'd seen? But she'd been shot, not knifed, and what about the bloody eagles? Did it all happen at the same time? But that wasn't how they usually worked. It was maddening not to know what was happening. He'd been getting sketchy reports, but he had no real idea what was happening, he hadn't just been watering it down for Sierra. It frustrated the hell out of him that he was no longer Kashena's backup. If he'd been there…

The Hummer hurtled down the road, both occupants praying to their own Gods that Kashena was okay.

Kashena lay in the hospital bed, her side bandaged. She was awake and she was stressing out. The man had said "this is for Jason" as plain as day. Was Jason in Los Angeles? Was he going after Sierra? What was happening? On top of that, how was Sierra going to react to this? Another injury? A more serious one this time.

She hadn't told Sierra about the vision, knowing it would only make things worse. She was at a complete loss as to how to fix what was wrong between them. She couldn't stop being a cop, and that meant she would keep getting hurt. Was this how it was meant to be? Was she meant to lose Sierra? Was losing Sierra what let her give up and die? She fully believed the vision she'd had, and that at the end of whatever was happening, she'd be dead. She knew she needed to make plans. She'd already started by taking out a life insurance policy for $2 million that would cover the house and any other bills that were left. Kashena had also contacted a lawyer to get her will in order; she knew it was morbid, but she felt that the vision had been sent for a reason. Hopefully it had been so she could get her affairs in order before it was over.

She was waiting to see if the man she'd shot and killed had indeed been a Marine. If that was the case, then it was likely the first part of the vision. He'd died bloody and she'd bled a great deal from her wound. Since the Marine symbol was an eagle, it would be the picture she'd seen.

Sebastian stepped into the room, relieved to see Kashena awake, and looking generally well. Sierra rushed past him and over to Kashena.

"Kash?" Sierra queried, her voice showing her strain.

"I'm okay," Kashena told her, her voice strong. "I need you to listen right now, okay?" Then she looked at Sebastian, "Colby?" she asked.

"On his way. I sent an officer for him."

"And you've confirmed he has him?" Kashena asked.

"Yes, just as we got to the hospital," Sebastian said, knowing that this was Kashena's way of coping with what was happening, making sure everyone she loved was safe.

Sierra looked perplexed at Kashena's words. "What do you mean listen to you, about what?" she asked, sounding lost suddenly.

"Sierra, the guy that shot me," she said, her tone strong. "He said, 'this is for Jason' before he did it."

"Oh my God…" Sierra said.

Sebastian closed his eyes where he stood, what she'd just said seemed to support the vision Kashena had.

"Jesus…" he breathed.

"So I need you to stay with Baz, no matter what, okay? You and Colby."

"What about you?" Sierra asked.

"I'll be okay," Kashena said.

The door to the hospital room opened then, and an officer spoke to Sebastian.

"Colby's here, so is Jericho," he said.

Kashena nodded. "Go check on Colby," she told Sierra, "I need to talk to Baz and Jericho."

Sierra looked surprised by the almost order-like quality of Kashena's direction, but nodded and left the room.

Sebastian told the officer to get Jericho, then he stepped over to where Kashena lay, helping her to sit up. She gasped at the pain that shot through her.

"You sure you're okay?" Sebastian asked.

"It's a through and through," she told him. "Just hurts like hell."

"How's the other guy look?" Sebastian asked.

"He looks dead," Jericho supplied from the doorway.

"Good," Sebastian said, his tone sure.

"Agreed," Jericho said as she walked over to them. "How are you doing Marshal?" she asked.

"I'm okay," Kashena said, nodding.

"So what happened?" Jericho asked.

"I was in the alley smoking," Kashena said. "He came up, asking for a cigarette. Big guy, but I didn't sense any kind of danger. I turned my head for a second and the next thing I know he's drawing down on me and says 'this is for Jason.' Before he can fire, I managed to skew his shot, and draw my weapon and return fire."

Jericho nodded. "Sounds like a clean shoot," she said.

"Yeah…" Kashena said, her tone raising the hair on the back of Sebastian's neck.

"What?" he asked, knowing his partner well.

Jericho looked between the two and knew she was seeing two people who knew each other backwards and forwards.

"This never makes it to Sierra's ears," Kashena said, her tone serious.

"Okay," Sebastian said, knowing he was about to hear something he didn't want to hear.

"He was going to kill me, Baz," she said. "He had that gun pointed at my head. He was there to execute me for Jason."

"Son of a fucking bitch…" Sebastian growled.

"Wait, who is Jason?" Jericho asked. "Is that Sierra's ex?"

"Yeah," Kashena said, nodding, "he should be at Folsom State Prison, but…"

"And Kash put him there," Sebastian added.

"Okay," Jericho nodded. "I'll get on the horn to corrections," she said.

"Jericho, I need Baz," Kashena said then. "He's the only person I trust to protect my family."

"You got it, no problem," Jericho said, pulling out her phone and walking to the door.

Kashena and Sebastian exchanged a look. Sebastian stepped over next to the bed, leaning in to gather his partner in his arms as carefully as he could, hugging her close. He knew they'd just taken another step toward her vision coming true. Someone was out to kill her and if her vision was right, and it had never been wrong before, he would succeed. It made Sebastian sick to even think about. Kashena was the only person in the world that was a constant in his life, and she meant everything to him. Losing her was not an option for him. It sucked to know that he might not have a choice in the matter.

Sierra and Colby came into the room, and Sebastian gave Kashena another gentle squeeze then let her go, stepping back out of the way. Sierra looked between them and knew she'd missed something, but Sebastian's look was impossible to read, as was Kashena's.

"Mom, are you okay?" Colby asked Kashena, stepping in to hug her carefully.

"Yeah, I'm alright," Kashena said, nodding.

"I'd like to hear that from an actual doctor," Sierra said, her tone reserved.

Kashena looked over at Sebastian, he nodded and left the room. Sierra knew that her wife and her partner's ESP was on as usual. A few minutes later Sebastian came back with the doctor in tow.

Kashena looked at her wife, then gestured to the doctor. Sierra turned to the man, with her most official look.

"I'm Assistant Attorney General Sierra Youngblood-Marshal," she said, extending her hand to the man. "You are?"

Kashena and Sebastian exchanged raised eyebrows. Apparently, Sierra had found it necessary to tell the doctor who she was, so he could be warned not to lie to her. A grin tugged at Kashena's lips. Leave it to her wife to diffuse any possible subterfuge in the most effective way possible. Fortunately for her and Sebastian, she hadn't been lying about being okay.

"Uh, Doctor Mark Johnson," the man said, glancing at his patient and then at the man who'd retrieved him rather abruptly.

"And you're my wife's doctor?" Sierra asked, gesturing to Kashena.

"I treated her, yes," the doctor said, nodding.

"And what is her condition?" Sierra asked, sounding like she was in a court of law.

"She's in fair condition," he said, nodding.

"Which means what, exactly?" Sierra asked, narrowing her dark eyes slightly.

Even Sebastian was grinning by this time, Kashena's wife meant business.

"It means that her vital signs are good, but she's likely still uncomfortable from her wound. We expect her to make a full recovery."

Sierra nodded, looking over at Kashena who smiled blissfully. Sierra narrowed her eyes at that smile.

"When will she get out of the hospital?" Sierra asked the doctor.

"We're going to keep her overnight to ensure there's no secondary infection, but barring that, she should be able to go home tomorrow."

"And how long should she stay off work to recover?" Sierra asked, shooting Kashena a triumphant look, even as Kashena rolled her eyes.

"Well, it depends on the patient," the doctor said, and saw the narrowing of Sierra's eyes again. "She should certainly stay down for at least three days," he said, hurriedly. "And her activities should be kept to a very minimal level for at least a week."

"Thank you," Sierra said, looking over at her wife again, her look saying, *Did you hear that?*

The doctor happily left the room then, and even Colby was grinning.

"Geeze Mom, you scared the crap outta that guy!"

"I just wanted the whole truth and nothing but the truth," Sierra said, looking over at her wife and her partner, who both did their best to look unassuming.

"You two should get home," Kashena said after a few minutes, looking over at Sebastian. "Baz is going to be with you."

"Why's Baz going to be with us?" Colby asked, his look confused.

Jericho walked back into the room, her look far from happy. She glanced at Sierra and Colby.

"It's okay," Kashena said to Jericho. "They need to hear whatever it is."

"He's out," Jericho said.

"What!" Sierra exclaimed, paling instantly.

"Baz!" Kashena shouted, as she practically leaped out of bed to move to Sierra's side, shredding her stitches.

"Whoa, whoa, whoa…" Sebastian said, moving to Kashena's side.

"Sierra?" Kashena queried softly, feeling blood start to drip down her side.

"Kash!" Sebastian bellowed, to get her attention. "She's fine, you on the other hand," he said, moving to pick her up and set her gently on the bed again. He moved her shirt to look at the bandaged wound. "Damn it Marine…" he muttered, pushing the call button for the nurse. Then he looked at Jericho, who'd watched the preceding with an odd look on her face.

The nurse came into the room. "Yes?" she queried.

"Can you get the doctor or someone to re-suture my stupid friend here?" Sebastian said, his most brilliant smile on full wattage.

The nurse moved past him to look at Kashena's side.

"Oh my, how did that happen?" the nurse asked, looking at Kashena.

"She's an ex-Marine," Sebastian said. "They can't keep shit closed to save their lives," he said, winking at Kashena.

"Shut it, Ranger," Kashena muttered.

"I'll get a PA," the nurse said, and scurried out of the room.

"Now, as you were saying?" Sebastian said, looking at Jericho and moving to sit next to Kashena, his way of keeping her from repeating the previous folly.

"Corrections paroled him for good behavior."

"Why weren't we notified?" Sierra asked, having regained her composure.

"Apparently, corrections hadn't updated your address yet and sent notification to your house in Sacramento."

"Jesus…" Kashena said, shaking her head.

"Fuckin' corrections," Sebastian growled.

"So where is he?" Sierra asked. "Do they even know?"

Jericho curled her lips in distaste. "They're going to do some checking," she said. "I informed them that we suspect he was involved in the attack on the police officer who was responsible for his previous arrest, so they've got a fire lit under their asses right now."

"Good," Sebastian said, nodding.

"Dad's out?" Colby asked, looking worried.

"Apparently," Sierra said to him, reaching out to pull him to her, hugging him. "Don't worry, Sebastian is going to take care of us, okay?"

"What about Kash?" Colby asked, worried.

"I'll be okay," Kashena said.

"I'll be leaving an officer here to keep an eye out," Jericho assured both Sierra and Colby. "No one's getting to her again," she said, her eyes on Colby.

Colby nodded, appreciating Jericho's assurances.

"Okay, let's go so Kash can rest," Sebastian said, moving off the bed as the physician's assistant came in with the supplies she needed to re-suture Kashena's wound.

Colby walked over to Kashena, leaning in to hug her, and kissing her cheek. "Love you," he said.

"Love you," Kashena replied, hugging him and kissing the top of his head.

Sierra moved in and kissed Kashena, her look still worried, and Kashena could sense the distance between them. Reaching out, she pulled Sierra to her, hugging her, and closing her eyes, wanting to will away the chill she felt in her soul. When she shifted, she hissed in pain and Sierra straightened instantly, her eyes pained and fearful. Sebastian leaned over kissing Kashena on the forehead.

"Rest partner, I've got them," he told her.

Kashena nodded, having to swallow a couple of times to try to get rid of the lump in her throat. After they left the PA re-sutured the wounds.

"Do you want more pain meds?" the woman asked, looking down at Kashena when she finished.

"Since I haven't had any, some to start with would be good," Kashena said, her tone wry. At the woman's confused look, she sighed, then nodded. "Yeah."

The PA put a shot into the IV in her arm. Kashena fell into deep dream filled sleep; her last conscious thought was to wonder how it felt to die.

Kashena was discharged from the hospital the next day. Sebastian showed up to drive her home, assuring her that Sierra and Colby were at home with two of his best officers watching them.

On the drive back to the house, Sebastian glanced over at her. He could see that she was still tired from whatever medication they'd given her in the hospital. It was obvious there was more to it than that, but he didn't want to push her.

Once at the house, Sebastian let Sierra settle Kashena in their bedroom. Sebastian watched as Kashena took a couple of the painkillers that the hospital had sent home with her. She wasn't given to using Western medicine, usually relying on holistic remedies. Then she settled down to sleep.

When she was asleep, Sebastian pulled a chair up close to the bed and sat down. It was obvious to Sierra that he intended to watch over his friend, quite literally.

The next day, Jericho called Sebastian to confirm that the man who had shot Kashena had indeed been a Marine, prior to going to prison at Folsom, where he had met Jason.

"Great," Sebastian muttered. "Where's Jason now?"

"Still in Sacramento, from what I'm told," Jericho said. "I'll keep checking back. Midnight's sent an inquiry to corrections to find out why Jason was released without notifying her office or his victims," Jericho said, her tone indicating she was quoting Midnight on that last part.

"Good," Sebastian said simply.

He took heart that Kashena's injury wasn't being taken like it was part of her job and that Midnight seemed to want some answers from corrections just as badly as he did. His partner would be dead right now if it wasn't for her lightning fast reflexes. It pissed him off.

A little later, Kashena woke up. Turning over onto her side she saw that Colby sat in the chair next to the bed.

"You got babysitting duty?" Kashena asked, her voice gravelly.

Colby looked up from the magazine he was reading. "Yeah," he said, with a grin. "Mom and Baz went down to her office for some meeting she couldn't miss."

"Lucky you," Kashena said, closing her eyes slowly, feeling the effects of the painkillers she was practically mainlining now.

"Ah, you're not so bad," Colby said. "You don't even snore."

Kashena chuckled. "Good to know."

"How are you feeling?" he asked, his dark eyes scanning her face.

"You look just like your mom when you do that," Kashena said, grinning sadly.

"Do what?" he asked, grinning.

"Check me over visually," Kashena explained.

"Baz said he'd kick my ass if there was a hair out of place on you when he got back," Colby said, his tone serious.

Kashena laughed outright at that, it definitely sounded like her partner.

"He's a bit over-protective where I'm concerned," Kashena said, by way of excuse for her partner's extreme orders.

"You'd protect him with your life too though, right?" Colby asked, although his tone really wasn't questioning.

"Right," Kashena said, nodding. "Just like I will for you and your mom."

"Will?" Colby asked, his look perplexed. "You mean, would right?"

"Right," Kashena said, nodding, thinking that painkillers really sucked for keeping ones tongue from misspeaking.

Colby nodded, then looked at her seriously.

"Do you really think my dad will come after us?" he asked, his real concern coming to bare.

Kashena looked back at him, trying to decide how much she wanted to say. He was definitely old enough now to understand how things were with his dad, but did she want to scare him?

"Well," Kashena began, her look conflicted.

"Tell me the truth, Mom," Colby said, his look direct.

Kashena was surprised by not only his words, but by his look.

"Okay," she said, inclining her head. "I think that your dad sees you and your mom as property of his that I've stolen. I think he wants you two back and he wants me dead."

Colby stared back at Kashena open mouthed. "He'd kill you?"

"Yes, I think he would." Kashena said honestly. "I think that's his plan."

Colby blinked a few times as he tried to assimilate this information.

"Col, you need to be there for your mom," Kashena said, reaching her hand out to touch his leg, her voice strained suddenly. "If something happens to me, you need to be there for her."

"Nothing is going to happen to you," Colby said, shaking his head, his tone petulant.

Kashena looked back at this handsome boy, who called her Mom, and her heart broke a little bit more. She couldn't control the tears that welled in her eyes at that moment. Even though she did her best to look away and force the tears away, she didn't quite succeed.

"You're afraid of him?" Colby asked, his voice worried now. "You think he can kill you?"

Kashena looked back at Colby, really wishing she could lie to him and say she didn't think that, but since her vision had shown her death, she didn't want to give him false hope. She wanted to prepare him. Because the words wouldn't come, she finally nodded.

Colby's eyes filled with tears, and Kashena felt a wave of grief and guilt that wanted to drown her. She reached out to him so she could bring him onto the bed to hug him. He hugged her as best he could as he cried, and Kashena's tears flowed as well.

"You know that I love you," Kashena said, her voice gruff with tears. "And you should know how proud I am of you, of the man you're becoming. Never forget that," she said, her voice breaking on the last word.

That had Colby crying harder, which just twisted the knife of guilt in her gut.

"I'm sorry," Kashena said to him when he finally quieted and sat back. "I didn't want to upset you, but I don't want to lie to you either."

Colby nodded. "You said you'd protect me and Mom with your life, well, I would protect you with mine."

"Colby, no," Kashena said immediately, her voice coming out more harsh than she'd meant it. "You can't," she said, shaking her head. "You have to be here for your mom. She can't lose you too."

"Too?" Colby repeated.

Damn it! Kashena thought.

"I meant if something happened to me," Kashena said, "she couldn't lose you too. So if anything happens, you need to run, do you understand me? You run, you get away from your father as fast as you can, do you understand?" Again her voice had taken on a sharp tone, but she needed to know that Colby wouldn't sacrifice his life for her.

It wouldn't matter anyway, she'd be dead and Sierra would be alone and it would be her fault. When Colby said nothing, Kashena narrowed her eyes at him.

"Tell me you understand, Colby," Kashena said, her tone serious.

Colby nodded, his look cowed. Kashena felt like shit for that, but she couldn't have him trying to be heroic and getting killed for it. She wasn't altogether sure that Jason wouldn't kill his son if he saw that he had more loyalty for Kashena than for him. She didn't want to find out.

A few minutes later, Sierra entered the room, and could immediately sense the tension.

"What's going on?" she asked.

"Nothing," Colby said. "I'm gonna go to my room," he said, standing up and leaving the room without looking back at Kashena.

Kashena's eyes followed him out of the room, her look tortured.

"What happened?" Sierra asked, her tone all 'mama bear' as Kashena liked to call it when Sierra was protecting her cub.

Kashena looked back at Sierra, once again feeling the pain of the distance between them.

"Kashena?" Sierra queried, her tone still strident.

Kashena shrugged. "Nothing, like Colby said," she said, moving to lie on her back and throwing her arm up over her eyes.

Sebastian walked into the room at that moment. He looked between Kashena and Sierra, knowing he was walking into something, feeling the tension still in the room. Sierra glanced at him, then back at her wife, shaking her head.

"I'm going to go talk to Colby," Sierra said, then left the room.

Sebastian moved to sit down in the bedside chair. "What did I miss?"

Kashena sighed, lifting her arm from her eyes. "My running off at the mouth, and poor Colby taking the brunt of it."

"Jesus, what did you say?" Sebastian asked.

"He said he'd protect me with his life, Baz," Kashena said, her tone sharp. "You think I could let him think like that? Knowing what I know?"

Sebastian's look closed off immediately. "You don't know anything," he said, his tone as sharp as hers.

"I got hundreds of ancestors that would beg to differ," Kashena said mildly.

"I don't fuckin' care, Kash, you don't know anything," Sebastian said, his voice angry.

Kashena looked back at him; she knew it was tearing him up to know that she was going to die and there wasn't anything he could do about it. She knew it was pissing him off. Fate had taken it out of his hands, somehow.

"It was death, that's all," Sebastian said. "It doesn't mean it's yours. It could be Jason's death."

Kashena smiled sadly at the vehemence in his voice. "Oh, but I do know that."

"How?" Sebastian said.

"It was the Ojibwa symbol for death, Baz, it wouldn't have shown that way if it was Jason's. Besides it was the symbol for a woman, and it was upside down, which means someone kills me."

Sebastian looked physically sick "I fucking hate your ancestors."

Again, Kashena just smiled sadly.

"What did you say to Colby?" Sierra asked, when she strode back into the bedroom a few minutes later.

"I'm gonna give you two some privacy," Sebastian said, and he walked out of the room.

"What did you say to him, Kash?" Sierra repeated.

"He asked me if I really thought Jason would come after you two, and I told him the truth."

"And what truth is that?" Sierra snapped.

"That I think Jason wants you two back and that he wants me dead," Kashena said, her tone matter-of-fact. What Sierra couldn't see was the knot that Kashena's guts were twisting into inside her.

"Jesus!" Sierra exploded. "Why would you tell him that?" she asked, her tone disbelieving. "Are you crazy?"

Kashena looked back at her wife, unable to formulate a reply that wouldn't lay bare every fear she had for them, and for herself. Finally she just shrugged. "Maybe."

"Great," Sierra replied sarcastically. "This," she said, pointing her finger downward, "this is the kind of thing that I can't deal with."

Kashena didn't reply, simply nodding instead.

"It's bad enough that I'm scared for you all the time now, but now you're scaring Colby…"

When Kashena didn't reply for a long moment, Sierra glowered at her.

"I don't know what you want me to say here," Kashena said, her voice indicating her frustration. "I'm a cop, Sierra. You married a cop, and cops get hurt and people target them, and shit happens, and I'm sorry, but I don't know how to stop all of that."

"You could stop being a cop," Sierra fired back.

"Really?" Kashena said, her voice strident. "It's that easy, what if I said that you should stop being a lawyer, Sierra? Could you do that?" she asked, already knowing the answer. "I'm a cop, I'm good at being a cop. And the only other thing I was ever good at was being a Marine," she said, her blue eyes flashing in anger. "So you fucking pick!"

Sierra stared back at her, like she didn't recognize who she was looking at. Finally, she shook her head and walked out of the room. Kashena lay panting with the effort to calm down, because getting so twisted up in anger had made her wound start to painfully throb.

"Fuck!" Kashena yelled, picking up a remote that lay nearby and hurled it across the room.

As Sebastian entered, he shifted back just in time to miss the hurtling object, watching as it smashed against the bedroom wall.

"Nice shot," he said, his tone even.

Kashena lay back, closing her eyes, trying to calm herself down.

Sebastian moved to sit down on the chair, his eyes on his partner. He knew there was a lot happening in her head, and now it sounded like she was fighting with her wife too. It wasn't a good direction for things.

"So what's going on?" he asked.

Kashena opened her eyes, looking over at him, then shook her head in disbelief.

"My life is falling apart around me," she said simply.

"With the counselor?" Sebastian asked. "I doubt that. She loves you."

Kashena gave a short sarcastic laugh. "Yeah, except the fact that I'm a cop."

Sebastian looked surprised. "Uh, she didn't know that when she married you?"

"I wasn't that kind of cop then," Kashena said, her tone snide.

"Only one kind…" Sebastian said.

"I guess she didn't get that memo," Kashena said, her tone tired. "She freaked out when I got bruised up last week … now this…" she said, indicating her wound.

Sebastian gave her a sardonic look. "She does realize that the reason you're hurt now is because of her, right?"

Kashena looked back at him, her look answering the question.

"She didn't get that memo either?" Sebastian asked, his tone wry.

"Guess not," Kashena said.

They were both quiet for a few minutes, then Kashena looked over at him. "I need to tell you some stuff," she said, her tone cautious.

Sebastian narrowed his green eyes. "What?" he asked.

Kashena blew her breath out, knowing he wasn't going to like what she was going to tell him, but she needed to tell someone she could trust.

"I took out a life insurance policy," she said, "for two million."

"Jesus Kash..." Sebastian breathed.

"Look, I need to make sure that she's taken care of," Kashena said, "and this house will break her without my income."

Sebastian shook his head. "I don't want to hear this."

"You need to hear it. She doesn't know about it and I can't tell her without telling her about the vision, and even if I did that, the fucking lawyer in her would make me give it up because I have prior knowledge of my death, or some stupid legal-eeze shit. I need you to help me here, Baz."

"To do what?" Sebastian asked. "To fucking help you die? Are you really asking me to do that, because I can't, I won't," he said, his tone strong.

167

"All you have to do is tell her about it when it's done, okay?" Kashena said. "And you have to be here for her, Baz, her and Colby… I need to know they're going to be okay."

Sebastian looked back at his best friend, he couldn't believe they were even having this conversation.

"Please Baz…" Kashena said, her voice constricted, because tears were clogging her throat again.

"Fine," he said, holding up his hand.

The last person whose tears he could handle was hers.

"Okay," Kashena said, nodding, as she reached for the bottle of painkillers.

"How many of those are you up to a day?" he asked, his eyebrow raised.

"Don't start with me," Kashena said.

"So I should let you kill yourself that way?" he asked, his tone even.

Kashena blew her breath out. "I need to sleep, so I don't think okay? Right now, I just need to not think."

"About what?" he asked.

"About how my marriage is likely on its way to being over and how that might be the reason I give up and let him kill me," Kashena said, her eyes flashing angrily.

"Jesus Kash…" Sebastian said, as she took two more of the pills.

"You asked," Kashena said, putting her arm up over her head again.

Sierra had noticed a very definite chill in Sebastian's eyes since the day they'd gone to the office and she and Kashena had fought. Since that day Sierra had been sleeping in another room, and she hadn't really gone in to talk to Kashena again. She was still angry about Kashena scaring Colby. Colby hadn't been willing to tell her what was said, but it was obvious from the way he'd been acting that he was really worried about something. Kashena's admission to what she'd said to him had made her so mad; she didn't think it was right that Kashena would put that onto Colby. Yes, Jason was probably dangerous, but murder? She didn't think that was something he'd stoop to. He'd been a Marine after all, and they had some modicum of honor.

After two days, Sierra decided she really should check on Kashena. She felt guilty that she'd been too afraid of fighting with her again to risk going into their room. When she walked in, Sebastian was reading a report. He glanced at her, his eyes icing over immediately, and she could feel the chill in the air. Kashena was, as usual these days, asleep with her arm thrown up over her head.

"She seems like she's sleeping all the time," Sierra commented softly.

Sebastian's look was wry as he raised his eyebrow at her. Reaching over, he picked up the bottle of painkillers and shook it. It was obvious there weren't a lot left. It had only been two days since Kashena had come home from the hospital.

Sierra looked back at him. "She's taken that many?" she asked a bit aghast.

Sebastian grinned icily. "Well, I'm not takin' them, sweetheart."

"Do we have a problem, Sebastian?" Sierra asked him, finally losing her temper.

"Yeah, we have a problem," he said, his tone sharp. "My best friend is drugging herself into a stupor, because her wife can't get her head wrapped around the idea that she married a cop two years ago and that cops get hurt."

Sierra stared back at him, surprised by his words.

"Drugging herself into a stupor?" Sierra repeated.

Sebastian gave her a quelling look. "When's the last time you saw Kash take painkillers, Sierra?" he asked, his look telling her that she knew the answer to that.

Sierra looked back at him, knowing he was right, and knowing she'd been purposely obtuse. She swallowed against the guilt that welled up in her throat. She shook her head slowly.

Sebastian watched Sierra try to reconcile her neglect of Kashena, and it only irritated him more.

"She," he said, jabbing his finger toward Kashena, "is the strongest person I've ever known," he said, his tone matching the anger in his eyes. "And you're fucking killing her with this bullshit. Only you could take her out like this." He stood up suddenly, driven to his feet by his anger and pain. He knew he needed to get out of that room or he was going to tell Sierra everything, and he knew Kashena wouldn't forgive him for that. He couldn't take the chance. He moved toward Sierra and saw her tense, as if he would hit her. To himself he thought, *Good, let her think that I just might,* as he moved past her and stalked out of the room.

Sierra stood still where she was, listening as Sebastian slammed the back door. She knew he'd be out there smoking for a while. She had thought that he was going to hit her. She knew Sebastian wasn't the kind of man to strike a woman, but she also knew that Kashena was the only thing in the world that meant everything to him, and for her sake, he might strike Kashena's wife. Sierra's eyes went to Kashena and to the bandage on her side. After a few minutes she sighed and left the room.

Colby found his mother sitting in the front room, staring at nothing.

"Mom?" he queried cautiously. He'd heard Sebastian yell earlier and then had heard him slam out of the house. He was worried.

Sierra looked at her son, then held out her arms to him. He moved to sit next to her, hugging her. Sierra held him in her arms, and closed her eyes.

Colby sat back after a few minutes, looking at Sierra.

"What's happening with you and Kash?" he asked.

Sierra grimaced, she hadn't meant for Colby to be affected by the fighting going on, but she realized that she couldn't keep it hidden from him. He was too old not to notice things anymore, like he'd been when she'd been married to Jason. Even then he'd heard and seen more than he should have.

"Things are kind of a mess right now," Sierra said.

"Because of Dad?" Colby asked.

"That's part of it," Sierra said. "But the other part is Kashena getting hurt doing her job."

"Why is that a mess?" Colby asked.

Sierra looked at him, and then sighed. "Because I worry about her, I'm afraid for her."

171

"She's afraid too, Mom," Colby said.

"No, Colby, she's not, that's what worries me."

"She is, Mom," Colby insisted. "She told me."

"What did she tell you?" Sierra asked. She was sure that he was going to tell her that Kashena thought that Jason was going to take them back and kill her. She was ready to explain to him that there was a difference in stating what one thought was going to happen, and actually being afraid of it.

"That she's afraid of Dad," Colby said. "And I told her that I'd protect her with my life," he said, and then lowered his eyes. "That's when she got mad at me."

Sierra was still trying to deal with what he'd said first, Kashena had told her son that she was afraid of Jason? Then it clicked in her head what he'd said after that.

"You said you'd protect her with your life, Colby?" Sierra asked.

He nodded his head, his eyes still downcast.

"And she got mad at you?" Sierra asked.

"She said that…" he began, tears choking his voice for a moment. "That you couldn't lose me too…" He raised his head, tears in his eyes that spilled over. "She really thinks Dad is going to kill her Mom, and she's scared…" His voice broke off again, as he put his arms around his mother, crying.

Sierra held Colby, her own tears flowing. *My God, my God* was all she could think.

Kashena woke, feeling like she was swimming through Jell-O. Shifting in her bed, she groaned out loud as the pain shot through her side.

"Painkillers my ass," she growled lowly to herself. "More like tranquilizers…"

She suddenly became aware of another person in the room and turned her head to see Sierra sitting next to the bed.

Sierra could almost feel the shield that dropped over Kashena's deep blue eyes. It pricked her conscience, and she knew it was her that had put that look in her wife's eyes.

"What is it, Sierra?" Kashena asked, her look both cautious and impatient.

Sierra canted her head slightly. "Why do you ask it that way?" she asked softly.

Kashena's eyes narrowed, her lips pursing in consternation. "Well, you're sitting there," she said, motioning to the side of the bed. "Not laying here," she said then, touching the empty spot on the bed to her right. "And you've got your lawyer face on," she said the last with a touch of anger.

Sierra stared back at her wife; she read so much in Kashena's eyes. Kashena's face reflected annoyance and impatience; it just didn't make it to her eyes. Sierra suspected that Kashena didn't want her to see the hurt, the fear or the regret. In truth, Sierra didn't want to see that either. It was that thought that caused the pained look on her face.

Kashena looked away from the expression on Sierra's face, knowing her time was up and that Sierra was about to lower the boom.

Sheer desperation had Kashena saying sharply, "Can we not do this right now?"

"Do what?" Sierra asked, wanting to say so much, but unable to come up with the right words at that moment.

"This," Kashena said impatiently, "I just... can't right now..." she said, reaching up to press the heels of her hands to her eyes.

"I'm sorry," Sierra said, shaking her head.

She saw Kashena's jaw tighten and she knew that she was not getting through. Leaning over, she reached out to take Kashena's hands away from her eyes. She looked down at her, searching. Kashena turned her head, looking away.

"I'm sorry," Sierra said again.

That had Kashena's head snapping around to look at her.

"What are you sorry for?" she asked, her tone pained. "Which part? Marrying me, or just—"

Sierra cut her off by pressing her lips to Kashena's, kissing her softly. When she pulled back, Kashena's look was wary.

"I'm sorry for that," Sierra said. Seeing Kashena's eyes take on the cynical look she hadn't seen in a really long time, she rushed on. "For that look in your eyes right now, Kashena. For putting that look and so many others back in your eyes."

Kashena looked back at her, and Sierra could read confusion on her face now.

"I'm sorry that you don't know what I'm talking about right now," Sierra said, smiling softly. "I'm sorry that you're waiting for me to say something that I can't say."

"What's that?" Kashena asked, her tone still tinged with fear.

"That I'm leaving you."

Kashena turned her head slightly, giving her a confused look. "You're saying that, or that you won't say that?"

Sierra blew her breath out in frustration. "For a litigator, I'm really failing at communication right now," she said, more to herself than to Kashena.

She leaned down to kiss Kashena's lips again, her lips trying to say what she couldn't manage to. For a moment she could feel Kashena soften, her hands reaching up to touch Sierra's face, then Kashena groaned and tore her lips away.

"Jesus, Sierra, tell me what you're saying," Kashena said, her voice ragged with emotion.

"I'm saying I love you, and I'm not going anywhere, ever," Sierra said. "I'm saying that I'm sorry I've put you through this with my stupid fears and worries. That I've been so—"

Kashena's lips on hers stopped her words. Kashena pulled her close, kissing her, her hands sliding through Sierra's hair, her lips moving over Sierra's with a mixture of hunger and tenderness. Within minutes though, she was wincing from the pain in her side. Sierra moved to lie next to her, levering herself up to look down at her wife.

"Colby told me what you said to him," Sierra said.

"What was that?" Kashena asked, her tone cautious.

"He said that you told him that I couldn't lose him too…" Sierra said, her voice trailing off.

"If things happen," Kashena said.

"I really don't think Jason would kill anyone, Kashena," Sierra said.

"And I think you're wrong," Kashena said softly.

"And you think he's going to kill you," Sierra said, her tone tremulous.

Kashena nodded.

"He was a Marine for God's sake," Sierra said.

"Is that the hope you're clinging to?" Kashena asked. "He was a Marine that raped his wife and hit her in front of their son… He's not the good kind of Marine, Sierra."

"And Colby said he'd protect you with his life," Sierra said.

"Yes, he did," Kashena said, her tone somber.

"He wants you to know how much he loves you, Kash…" Sierra said, her voice sad.

"And I love him, Sierra, that's why I can't take the chance that he'll try to be a hero," she said, her look very serious. "Heroes die."

Sierra looked back at her, shocked, then she grimaced. "Then what does that make you? When you protect us with your life."

Kashena looked back at her, still serious. "A hero."

Chapter 7

Raine was lying next to Natalia, they were both sleeping when a phone began ringing.

Raine groaned as she turned over looking at her phone. "Babe, it's you."

Natalia reached past Raine, picking up her phone and looking at it. She picked up the call.

"Si?" she said, listening, smiling and nodding. "Great! Gracias!"

"What was that?" Raine asked, moving to pull Natalia back to her.

"I have an interview later today," Natalia said, snuggling back into Raine's arms.

"You're quitting the gym?" Raine asked, surprised.

"No," Natalia said, shaking her head. "This is for a second job."

"How are you going to hold down two jobs and go to school?" Raine asked.

"Well, I may have to take less classes," Natalia said.

"But that'll take you even longer to get your degree," Raine pointed out.

Natalia looked back at her, smiling, "I'll still get it," she said, shrugging.

"Why do you need a second job?" Raine asked.

"Because I can't afford this apartment without it," Natalia said.

"How much is your rent?" Raine asked.

"Twenty-five hundred," Natalia answered. "I've used up my savings trying to keep up."

"So, what if it was twelve fifty a month?" Raine asked.

"How would that happen?" Natalia asked.

"If you have a roommate," Raine said.

"It's a one bedroom," Natalia said. "You want me to have another girl here?"

"No, I want to be the girl here."

"You'd do that?" Natalia asked surprised.

"Are you actually asking me that?" Raine asked, equally surprised.

"Well, I didn't know…" Natalia said.

"I'm here, most of the time anyway," Raine said. "I might as well pay rent," she said, grinning.

"But I thought you liked your apartment."

"I do. But I like being here with you more," Raine said. "Or did you not want that…" she asked, suddenly realizing that Natalia may not have wanted that.

"Way past the second date, mija," Natalia said, grinning.

"Oh," Raine replied, grinning. "So when is your rent due again?"

"End of the week," Natalia said. "But I know you need to give notice and everything."

"I'll pay the whole thing on Friday," Raine said.

"What? No," Natalia said. "That's not right."

Raine leaned in kissing Natalia's lips. She pulledback to look into her eyes. "I'm doing it."

"Why?"

"Because I want to, and because I love you," Raine said, smiling. "I'll move in this weekend."

"But don't you need to give notice?"

"Are you saying you don't want me here this weekend?"

"You'll lose so much money!" Natalia exclaimed.

"I haven't used my savings up," Raine said, grinning.

"Callate," Natalia said, narrowing her eyes and telling Raine to, *Shut up*.

Raine chuckled.

"Are you sure you can afford to do this?" Natalia asked.

"Yes, I'm sure," Raine said, glancing at the clock and seeing that it was still early. "Make sure you call whoever that was back and cancel that interview."

Natalia looked up at her, ever amazed by this woman. For someone who'd never been in a relationship before, she certainly understood the idea of a partnership.

This was further proven the following weekend when Raine moved in.

To Natalia's shock, Raine only had a few boxes of things. They were standing in Raine's bedroom at her apartment. Raine gestured to the pieces of furniture that she had.

"Do you want, or need any of this stuff?" she asked.

Natalia was surprised by the question. Raine's furniture was far nicer than her own furniture. She'd figured that Raine would put it in storage. Suddenly she realized Raine was looking at her expectantly.

"I, um," Natalia stammered.

"What?" Raine asked, knowing that somehow she's surprised Natalia again, but not knowing how this time.

"I just figured you'd put stuff in storage or something…" Natalia said, her voice trailing off as she shrugged.

Raine looked back at her for a long moment, her look perplexed. "Why?"

Natalia's brows furrowed with bewilderment. "For when…" she began, then stopped herself.

Raine looked back at her for a long moment, then understanding dawned.

"For when we break up and I go back to my own place," Raine said her look pointed. "Right?"

Natalia pressed her lips together, knowing that for Raine it was a terrible way to think, but Natalia had been through enough relationships to know how things happened sometimes.

Raine shook her head. "How can you be in a relationship and already be planning for the end?"

"Because there's always an end," Natalia said simply.

Raine just looked back at her, her look somewhere between disappointed and sad. Finally she nodded. "So, yes or no on the furniture?"

It took Natalia a few moments to catch up, she nodded. "Okay, sure," she said, not understanding Raine's mood, but not wanting argue about it.

Three hours later they'd moved everything in and set it up. Raine went in to take a shower. Natalia sat on the bed they'd just set up and made and looked around at the room. It was much improved with Raine's furniture, and not her pressboard stuff that she'd picked up at Walmart or wherever. Raine's furniture was solid wood, and good quality. It seemed that she spent money on what she thought mattered.

After Raine got out of the shower and got dressed, she walked back into to the bedroom.

"Let's go," she said.

"Go?" Natalia asked. "Where?"

"Well, we need a TV for the living room, and definitely need more than just the one couch, and whatever else you like."

"But…" Natalia began, she didn't have money for that kind of stuff at that point.

"Let's go," Raine said, holding her hand out to Natalia.

Finally Natalia took Raine's hand, but still wasn't sure how to broach the subject of her lack of funds.

As it turned out, the question never came up. Raine paid for everything without ever even looking at Natalia like she expected her to. When they looked at furniture, for the living room, Raine liked a set of recliners that were expensive to Natalia's way of thinking.

"Do you like them?" Raine asked her. The same question she'd asked about the paintings they'd picked out for the living room.

"Si, que estan bien," Natalia said, *Yes they are very nice*. "Pero caro," she said then, saying, *But they are expensive*, trying not to offend the hovering saleswoman.

"You get what you pay for, babe," Raine said, winking at her. "We'll take them," she said to the saleswoman.

"Fabulous!" the woman said.

On the way home in the car, Natalia looked over at Raine.

"Why did you buy all of that?" Natalia asked.

Raine looked over at her. She was driving Natalia's car, as she often did now whenever they rode together and it wasn't feasible for them to take the motorcycle.

"We needed it," Raine said.

"No, we didn't need it," Natalia said, her tone neutral.

"Okay, we didn't need it," Raine said. "But I just thought I should do my share."

"Your share is half of the rent, Raine," Natalia pointed out.

"Do you usually let women come live with you?" Raine asked, her tone conversational.

"What do you mean?" Natalia asked, surprised by the question.

"I mean, do you usually have women live with you? As opposed to you going to live with them."

"I always keep my apartment."

Raine nodded, accepting that answer. "So it's safer that way, right?"

"Safer?" Natalia asked, her tone cautious.

"Safer for you," Raine qualified.

Natalia looked back at Raine, trying to decide if she was being insulted or complimented.

Raine noted the conflict on Natalia's face and reached over to take her hand.

"You've been hurt in the past, and you've been let down by women you counted on and loved. It's completely understandable, Talia."

"You're saying that I keep my apartment so they can't take that away from me too," Natalia said.

"Exactly," Raine said, nodding.

Natalia smiled softly. "I guess that's probably true. It also keeps one constant in my life."

Raine nodded. "Well, that's why I pay more money for things that are better quality. I want something constant that will be around for a long time."

Natalia looked back at Raine and saw in that moment the way Raine saw things. She'd had nothing constant her entire life, except for change and... and Auri. And Auri had been taken away from her. Suddenly Natalia felt tears sting the backs of her eyes.

Raine was trying to make her a permanent part of her life, and she was already pushing her away by talking blithely about storing things for when they broke up, because things always end. She realized in that moment how much she'd hurt Raine earlier in the day. Raine was giving up her apartment, her constant, to help Natalia and for that she was getting Natalia's cynical outlook on relationships. And in the face of Natalia's doubt and callous disregard, Raine had remained the kind, generous person she always was.

"You are an amazing person, Raine Mason" Natalia said, taking Raine's hand between both of hers and leaning over to kiss Raine's shoulder.

Raine looked over at her, obviously unclear where the comment had come from, but smiling in appreciation for the kind words.

"You're kind of cute too," Raine said, making Natalia laugh, and lightening the mood in the car immediately.

It was that conversation that Natalia was thinking about in her class a few days later when she got a call. She was just leaving class when it came in, so she answered it without even looking at who it was.

"Yes?" she answered.

"Wouldn't count on your cop being home for dinner," said a voice on the other end, then the phone disconnected.

Natalia stopped dead in her tracks, looking at the display on the phone, but not seeing anything. Immediately she dialed Raine's cell phone number, but there was no answer. Natalia's blood ran cold as she started to run to the school parking lot. She got to her car only to find that the tires were all flat. She knew it had to be Julie. She wouldn't really do anything crazy, would she? *Yes, yes she would!* Natalia thought.

Natalia called Cat's phone next, and she answered on the second ring.

"Nat? What's up?" Cat queried, seeing Natalia's name on her phone display.

"It's Raine, she's in danger!" Natalia exclaimed. "I got a call, it said she wouldn't make it home for dinner… Catalina, it's Julie, she's going to hurt her. I can't get ahold of her, please help me…"

"Okay, Nat, calm down, Raine just left, she probably didn't answer her cell because she was on the bike and can't hear it. I'll get a patrol officer to track her down, okay? Calm down."

"Okay, okay," Natalia was practically chanting, sitting on the back bumper of her car and rocking back and forth in worry.

Raine was just getting onto the freeway when she noticed the red Honda following far too closely. It wasn't out of the ordinary, because asshole drivers did it all the time, but the fact that it was a red Honda caught her attention. Raine changed lane, and glancing back she saw that the windows were all dark, even the windshield had a tint. It wasn't a good sign. The Honda changed lanes too, getting behind her again and edging ever closer.

Raine glanced around her. In front of her traffic was flowing well, no slowdown to keep her speed down. There were a few big rigs on the road; she made note of where they were in the lane. She heard the whine of an engine being pushed and glanced in her mirror to see that the Honda was inching closer still.

Before it happened, Raine knew where it would come from. The Honda's engine gunned once more, and right as it caught up, veered over into the other lane giving Raine's back tire just the slightest tap. Raine tried to veer before the car made contact, but she wasn't fast enough. The bike wobbled and she fought it to keep it up right, feeling it starting to slide and go down. She knew she couldn't get caught under it; over five hundred pounds of bike on her leg would crush it.

Praying that the Honda didn't decide to finish the job by hitting her too, she let go of the bike, letting it go down, as she tumbled onto the pavement. Inside her helmet she shut her eyes, because she had no control over what was happening now. She felt her helmet hit the pavement, and saw stars instantly as the pain exploded in her head. She reached a hand out to try and stop her forward motion, but realized too late that it was a bad idea. She yanked her arm up as the skin was ripped off her forearm. That's when she saw red and thought for sure that the Honda was indeed going to hit her now. *Damnit!* was the last thing she thought before everything went dark.

She came to in the ambulance, and heard the EMT saying something about helmets. Her head hurt too much to focus on what was being said. She blacked out again, thinking that someone needed to turn that damned siren off…

"Jesus…" Cat said, seeing the wreckage of the Shadow.

"Yeah, that's never pretty," said the patrol officer who'd been the first on the scene.

Cat nodded. The Shadow was a hulk of twisted metal. Cat heard a shriek and turned just in time to catch Natalia who had lunged toward the wreck.

"Woah!" Cat yelled and she grabbed hold of Natalia. She was crying hysterically and trying to wiggle out of Cat's grasp, her eyes glued to what was left of the Shadow. "Natalia! Hold on!" Cat yelled, having to use all of her strength to detain the smaller girl, who was actually solid muscle, even if it was lean muscle. It was everything Cat could do to hold on to her.

"Ella esta murete?" Natalia was asking, her voice stricken.

"No, she's not dead," Cat answered, knowing enough Spanish to understand what Natalia said. "She was taken to the hospital and I'm going to take you there now, okay?"

Natalia had to tear her eyes away from the wreckage. She looked at Cat with tears streaming down her cheeks, finally nodding as what Cat had just said sunk in.

The drive to the hospital was quick, and Natalia looked terrified the entire time. At one point, Cat reached over taking Natalia's hand in hers, squeezing it gently. She knew what it was like to be afraid someone you loved was dying as you were trying to get to the hospital. Cat had experienced that with Kana, and then had experienced worse when her ex-girlfriend had been kidnapped. She'd had no idea what condition they'd recover her in or if she'd be alive at all.

At the hospital, Cat left her car in the front of the emergency room and walked Natalia in. She went straight to the front counter.

"An officer of mine was brought in, her name is Raine Mason, she was in a motorcycle accident. I need to know where she is."

"Are you family?" the woman asked.

"Yes, yes I am," Cat said, winking over at Natalia, thinking to herself, *Did you hear what I said at all?*

"She's in bed one twenty-four. The doctor is in with her now," the woman said.

Cat took Natalia's hand and led her down the hallway, looking for the right bed number. They came to the curtained off area that signified bed 124. Cat took a deep breath and pulled open the curtain. She just about passed out in relief to see Raine sitting on the bed, with a bandage on her arm and some scrapes and bruises. She wasn't hooked up to any machines or monitors.

Raine turned her head, grimacing as she did, but smiling at Natalia and Cat.

"Raine!" Natalia said, running straight over and into Raine's arms.

"I'm okay, honey, I'm okay," she said over and over, hugging Natalia to her as the other girl cried.

Cat looked at the doctor. "How's my girl?" she asked him.

The doctor looked confused for a moment, so Cat pulled her badge out of her pocket. "She works for me."

The doctor nodded, adjusting his glasses. "Ms. Mason will be just fine. She's suffered a concussion from hitting the ground, but her helmet saved her life. She has some contusions and abrasions, but other than that she will be just fine."

"Thanks, doc," Cat said, smiling at him.

The doctor left the room and Cat walked over to Raine, extending her hand to the other woman.

"Good to see you alive," Cat said.

"Thanks," Raine said, grinning.

"Your bike is trashed though," Cat said.

Raine nodded. "Yeah, I kinda figured."

"Raine, I got a phone call, it was a threat…"

Raine looked back at Natalia. "It was Julie," she said simply.

"You're sure?" Natalia asked, still unable to believe Julie would go this far.

"I know," Raine said. "It was her red Honda," she said, looking over at Cat. "I checked her out after that incident with her friend Jake.

She has a red Honda Accord, nineteen ninety-nine, plate number would be three D X A seven six five. Check it out. It should have some blue paint on it from the contact she made with my back fender."

Cat nodded, looking pleased as she pulled out her phone and walked toward the curtain to leave them alone.

"I was so scared," Natalia said, looked at Raine, still standing in the circle of her arms.

"Well, there's no reason to be scared now, I'm okay."

"She could have killed you!" Natalia exclaimed, her voice forceful.

"I know, honey, but she didn't, and that's what counts."

Natalia breathed a frustrated sigh. "I can't believe she did that..." she said, shaking her head.

"It does seem like a kind of crazy thing to do," Raine agreed. "Maybe she just doesn't like to lose."

"She had to believe that it would kill you," Natalia said. "How could she not?"

Raine could see Natalia wrestling with the thoughts as they came to her. She waited, knowing there was nothing she could say. Then she saw it click in Natalia's head.

"She was trying to kill you," Natalia breathed, her eyes widening in shock.

Raine's look confirmed what she'd said.

"You knew that," Natalia said.

"Yeah, I knew that," Raine confirmed. "You don't tap someone on a motorcycle like that if you don't expect them to end up dead. She was counting on it and she was counting on it looking like an accident."

"But you 'checked her out'?" Natalia asked.

"Yeah, I ran her through the system. You should know that she's had more than one restraining order against her by ex-girlfriends. I was also able to find out what vehicles she owns. That's how I knew about the Honda."

"She's had restraining orders against her?" Natalia asked, paling slightly.

"Yeah…"

Cat walked back into the area again, still on her phone, nodding in affirmation to whoever she was talking to.

"Great, thank you," she said, hanging up. "They picked Julie up, she's claiming she knows nothing about the attack."

"Of course she is," Raine said. "Did they get the car?"

Cat shook her head. "She ditched it somewhere. We'll find it, don't worry."

Raine nodded. "She wasn't counting on me still being alive to tell anyone anything, but she's smarter than I thought."

"Don't worry about it," Cat said. "You go home and get some rest. I've got an officer outside to drive you."

Raine nodded, moving to stand.

An hour later, Raine lay on the bed in their apartment. She hurt literally everywhere and honestly felt like she'd been hit by a truck. The hospital had sent her home with painkillers, but she was resisting taking them. She'd hated the way painkillers had made her feel after the explosion. Natalia walked into the bedroom, seeing Raine lying on the bed. Her eyes took in the beauty of this woman she had almost lost that day. Her rich red hair was loose around her. It was a rare occasion, only because Raine said the weight of it in a ponytail was making her head hurt more. She was wearing the least amount of clothing she could; a black exercise bra and shorts. The bruises and scrapes were evident on her body. One arm was bandaged where her jacket had ripped away allowing the pavement to slice open her arm.

It amazed Natalia that Raine was okay. Having seen the wreck her bike had been in, she'd been convinced that Raine would either be dead, or seriously injured. She'd expected to arrive at the hospital to have to wait for hours and hours while Raine was in surgery. The last thing she'd expected to find was Raine sitting up, looking almost completely normal.

Walking over to the bed, she saw Raine open her light blue eyes.

"How are you?" Natalia asked, handing Raine the water she'd asked for.

"My head hurts," Raine said. "Well, technically everything hurts right now."

Natalia grimaced. "Did you take one of those?" she asked, pointing at the bottle of pills from the hospital.

Raine shook her head.

"Porque no?" Natalia asked, wanting to know, *Why not*?

"I don't like how they make me feel," Raine said.

"They should make it so you don't hurt anymore," Natalia said gently.

Raine still looked hesitant.

"How did they make you feel?" Natalia asked, trying to approach the subject from a different angle.

"Like I was out of control," Raine said. "Too out of it to do anything."

"What do you need to do?" Natalia asked.

Raine shook her head, indicating that Natalia didn't understand. "It's not that, it's that I don't feel safe when I'm like that."

"Safe from what?" Natalia asked.

Raine didn't answer, she just shook her head again.

Natalia touched her cheek, her eyes looking up into Raine's. "I am here with you," she said softly, "you are safe."

Raine looked back at her. "But Julie…"

"Is in jail, remember?"

"But her friends," Raine said then.

"I will stay right here with you, I won't leave the apartment," Natalia said. "So nothing can happen to me. Okay, baby? Please take one of these so you can be out of pain," she said, holding up the bottle of painkillers.

Raine looked like she was debating her options, but finally nodded.

"You won't leave the apartment," Raine confirmed.

"I promise," Natalia said, nodding.

"Okay," Raine said. She took the pill that Natalia handed her with some water.

Natalia lay down next to her, and reached up to stroke Raine's arm gently. Then she touched her cheek, and moved her hand back into Raine's hair, soothingly. Within minutes Raine was asleep. Natalia smiled, still amazed that Raine had come through the accident with so few injuries. She knew that it had been Raine's skill at knowing how to fall on the bike, and also a good dose of luck, that had saved her. Natalia thanked God for his protection.

* * *

Kashena joined Sebastian out on her back patio as the sun was going down. She sat down, with a beer in her hand and lit a cigarette.

"Things between you and the little woman seem back on track," Sebastian said, grinning.

It had been two days since Kashena and Sierra had made up.

"I'm betting you have something to do with that," Kashena said, her look mild.

Sebastian shrugged. "She was being stupid."

"Stupid?" Kashena asked with a raised eyebrow.

"She was wasting the time she has with you," he replied, his expression fixed.

"Is that time she has left?" Kashena asked.

Sebastian narrowed his eyes at her. "Don't start that shit with me Marine…" he said.

Kashena canted her head, knowing that he didn't want to think about what was coming, but his words were telling. She knew that he was starting to accept what she'd seen; something inside her shifted at that point and she knew there was no hope. There was a calm that settled over her, and she knew that she would let things happen the way they were meant to now. No fighting, other than to ensure Sierra and Colby were safe in the end.

Sebastian saw something click in Kashena's head, and he swallowed against the lump that rose in his throat. Part of him wanted to grab her and run as far away from Los Angeles as they could get, but he knew she would never go, not with Sierra and Colby there to watch over. He steeled himself with the knowledge that it was his responsibility to make sure that Kashena's wife and son were safe, no matter what. That would be the best he could do for his friend and it made him sick to the very core.

Three weeks later, nothing had happened. It was relatively quiet. They had found nothing more on the Marine that had attacked Kashena, other than he'd been in a cell with Jason for a while. Regardless, Kashena checked with corrections every day to see where they had Jason located. She also got Jericho to leave Sebastian on Sierra's detail. In order to do so she'd had to tell Jericho about the vision. It had caused the director a lot of concern, but she, like Sebastian, hoped Kashena was wrong. Even so, she'd assigned Sebastian to the protection of Assistant AG Youngblood-Marshal "until further notice."

Driving home, Kashena always had at least an hour to keep working via her cell phone. She usually used every minute of that hour, or more finishing up things from the office. She'd managed to send three of her five troublemakers back to their departments, but she was still interviewing individuals to get the right fit for the unit. She was trying to track down one of the individuals she was particularly interested in hiring. This woman had been a Military Intelligence Officer, so she was very familiar with establishing contacts and working with informants. She worked for the Los Angeles Police Department, but had thus far been difficult to get ahold of to set up an interview. Kashena wanted to talk to her personally to see how she'd fit into the unit, but she felt she could only do that by meeting them in person.

Her phone rang just as she got to a very wooded area of the canyon road she was on. She was reaching to pick up the call, seeing that it was the woman she'd been trying to get ahold of, when she suddenly saw the black SUV coming up on one side of her. She was used to vehicles passing on this particular road, since it was a two-lane road and some people were impatient, but something told her this wasn't the case now.

She had just enough time to brace as the SUV suddenly swerved hitting her car and shoving it toward the shoulder. Kashena accelerated to try and get away, and she disconnected the woman's call and dialed Sebastian. She pulled ahead of the SUV but they were now pursuing her.

"Son of a bitch…" she muttered to herself, as the SUV pulled up alongside her again. This time she slammed on her brakes, putting her vehicle behind theirs. Unfortunately the SUV braked just as quickly and the front end of her car, a Mercedes SL550, slammed into and went under the SUV's high back end.

"Yeah?" Sebastian answered his phone, immediately hearing the screech of metal as the hood of the Mercedes twisted in the impact.

"Baz, it's happening, watch them!" Kashena had time to yell, before the car door was yanked open and she was hit on the head.

On his end, Sebastian yelled into the phone, "Kash!?" He heard a thud and the phone clatter to the ground then the call cut out. "Goddamnit!" he yelled.

He strode into the house, holding his phone and picking up the house phone.

"What's happening?" Sierra asked, looking worried.

Sebastian held up a finger to tell her to hold on, as he called the police dispatcher and asked her to trace the call, giving her the pertinent details.

"Oh my God…" Sierra breathed hearing what Sebastian was telling the dispatcher.

Unfortunately the call had disconnected too soon for them to trace.

"Fuck!" Sebastian yelled in sheer frustration. Looking at Sierra he said, "Get Colby."

Sierra nodded, heading upstairs to get her son. Her mind was going in a million different directions, she had no idea what to think. All she knew was that Kashena had been in a wreck and had called Sebastian to say 'it was happening.' She wasn't sure what that meant, but she was sure it had something to do with Jason.

Sebastian was on the phone immediately to Kashena's office trying to determine when she'd left. He was told it had been over an hour. He checked traffic patterns, seeing Colby come downstairs with Sierra. They both looked terrified.

"She was close, she was close…" he said to himself seeing that traffic had been heavy in one area, but other than that she wouldn't have been delayed.

He was on his phone again, calling the California Highway Patrol asking them to check out the canyon road for a wreck and that he had an officer down. Then he looked at Sierra and Colby.

"I don't know a lot yet," he told them, "but Kash called to say that something was happening. I heard a wreck, but it seems like she was close to home. I need both of you to make sure all the doors and windows are locked, and do not call anyone right now, or," he looked at Colby, "post on any social media."

Colby nodded, as did Sierra. They both moved to do what he'd asked.

A half an hour later, Kashena's car had been found by CHP. It was indeed wrecked. Her phone had been found at the scene, and there was blood on the driver's seat. CHP sent Sebastian a video of the scene. There was no second vehicle, so apparently whatever car Kashena had hit, had still been drivable.

"She went under something big," Sebastian said, looking at the video on his laptop while talking to the CHP officer. "Check for any reports in the area, it'd have to be a big SUV for the SL to go under like that and the truck to still be drivable. There's not a lot of blood, so it looks like they took her alive," he said, lowering his voice so Sierra didn't hear.

It wasn't a lot of consolation that she'd been taken alive, because it didn't mean they intended to keep her that way.

Sierra had contacted Jericho to let her know what was happening, and Jericho was getting on the phone to corrections to see what was happening with Jason, and if he was still in Sacramento. Sierra told Jericho that when Kashena had called about him the day before, she had been told he was still in Sacramento. So what had changed? Or was Jason not involving himself? That was the question.

***

Kashena woke to a throbbing in her head and coming to she realized she was somewhere dark, dank and wet. She was relieved to note that she wasn't bound in any way. These people were awfully confident, she thought to herself. She pushed herself up into a sitting position, feeling her vision swim a bit. Resting her head against the post behind her, she closed her eyes to wait for the feeling to pass.

She wondered if Sebastian had found her car yet. She knew he'd be freaking out, but she hoped that he also remembered the one thing she'd wanted from him was that he protect her family. As far as she was concerned her fate was sealed. As long as Jason didn't get to Sierra and Colby, she could let go.

It was at least another hour until she heard the door to the room open. She'd taken the time to walk around the room to determine if there was any way out. There were no windows, only a door that was locked from the outside. She'd attempted to pull at it a few times, but it didn't budge. Finally, she'd sat back down when her head protested her movement too much. She was sitting with her knees up to her chest when a man entered. She immediately moved to stand, her look wary. The man was tall, at least six foot, probably taller. He was burly and had short cropped blond hair and deeply tanned skin. Again, Kashena's first thought was *Marine?*

"You fucked with the wrong people, bitch," the man practically spat.

Kashena's face remained impassive except for a slight grin. "Happens a lot," she said, her tone apathetic.

"You won't have to worry about that for long, sweetheart," the man said, his grin sneering.

"I don't find myself too concerned," Kashena said, knowing she was baiting the man, but wanting him to come closer so she'd have a chance to take him down.

"You should be," he said, his tone serious. "You should never fuck with a Marine's wife."

Kashena canted her head slightly. "Neither should you."

"What the fuck does that mean?" the man snapped.

"It means that if you mess with my wife, you're fucking with a Marine's wife," Kashena said.

The man stared back at her openmouthed, but then he started to look cynical.

She took her DOJ windbreaker off her shoulders and down to her elbows, showing him the Marine tattoo on her upper left arm. His eyes widened as he looked from the tattoo to Kashena's face.

"What the fuck?" he muttered.

"Jason didn't tell you who you were after?" Kashena asked, her tone caustic. "Yeah, that sounds about right. Did he tell you I'm a cop? Or did he leave that part out too?" she asked, pushing her temporary advantage.

The guy was shaking his head, stepping back and holding his hands up.

"He said you trumped up charges on him so you could take his wife away from him."

"Yeah, he lied to you."

"He said you're a dirty cop."

"Sounds like he doesn't like me, I'm hurt," Kashena said, smiling now.

The man stared back at her, his eyes cautious now.

"Why don't you just be smart and let me go?" Kashena said her tone reasonable. "You already wrecked a sixty thousand dollar car, we could just leave it at that."

The man started shaking his head immediately. "I need to…" he began, and then turned and walked quickly out of the room.

Kashena heard the lock click, even so she went to check the door. It was indeed locked again.

"Damnit," she muttered.

Walking back over to the post she slid down it into a sitting position again. She hoped that she had put enough doubt in the man's mind to make him re-think working with or for Jason.

By nightfall, Sebastian had made no progress in finding Kashena. There had been a report of a black SUV speeding on the canyon road and the person had gotten a couple of numbers on the plate, but nothing really useful. Black SUVs were a dime a dozen in LA. His agitation level was at an all-time high. He knew that Jason could be killing Kashena at that moment and he would have no way of stopping it. What kept running through his mind was that they'd just find her body lying in a ditch somewhere and that would be the end of it. It wouldn't be the end of it, though; Sebastian would personally track Jason down and kill him slowly and painfully if that happened.

He stepped out onto the patio to smoke, moving to sit in one of the patio chairs. He was dying for a beer or something much stronger, but he didn't want to dull his senses, he knew Kashena was counting on him. In his mind he was running over the few things they knew. Jericho had come back with the information that corrections had gone into the house they thought Jason to be in, only to find that he wasn't actually there.

"Those people should be shot," had been Sebastian's reply.

"Trust me, Midnight will hear about this, and she will go after them, but it doesn't really help us now. We can count on Jason being in town," Jericho had said.

Knowing that they no longer had a bead on Jason, Sebastian knew things were definitely moving in the direction that Kashena had expected. She had always suspected that it would be Jason who killed her, but Sebastian really hoped she was wrong.

The slightest movement to his left caught his attention, and a second later he was knocking over the chair he sat in as he vaulted to his feet. The black-clad man charged at his mid-section, knocking Sebastian over the toppled chair.

"Son of a bitch!" Sebastian yelled, as he grappled with the man.

Kashena was pacing a few hours later when the door opened again. She was not surprised to see Jason walk through it. She was pleased to note that he did not look happy.

"Jason…" Kashena said. "Long time no see," she said sarcastically.

"Shut the fuck up!" Jason yelled, his frustration making the veins in his neck bulge.

"Why don't you come over here and make me?" Kashena said, her tone challenging. Then she raised an eyebrow. "Or are you afraid you can't?"

"Oh I can shut you up, bitch," he said, pulling out a gun. "But I don't have to get near you to do it."

Kashena looked at the gun, thinking in her head, *Not a knife.* "Kind of a chicken shit way to handle things, but okay."

"I said shut up."

Kashena's lips curled into a sardonic grin, her look superior and her blue eyes sparkling at the challenge.

"Think you're so fucking smart?" Jason said. "Think that big Ranger fucker can protect Sierra? Huh?" he asked, gleefully.

Kashena's chin came up at the mention of both Sebastian and Sierra, and her face grew serious as she said, "Leave them the fuck out of this, Jason."

"No, I don't think I will," he said, looking pleased with himself again. "Stupid fucking cunt, think you can take what's mine and get to keep it? No, I don't think so," he said, and with that he shot her in the leg.

Kashena fell to the floor, groaning. "Just fucking kill me Jason, and leave Sierra and Colby alone, move on with your fucking life!"

Jason walked over to her, grabbing a handful of blond hair and yanking her half off the floor, bringing her face close to his.

"Oh, I'm going to fucking kill you, bitch, but now I'm gonna make Sierra and Colby watch!" He let her go, and she fell to the floor in a heap.

He left the room then, and Kashena lay bleeding on the floor thinking Jason had just conjured up her worst nightmare.

Sebastian managed to get disentangled not only with the man who'd run at him, but the chair they'd both fallen over, ending up with the chair between them. Lashing out with his foot, he kicked the chair at the man, who ducked to miss it. Sebastian charged him, landing on top of him and throwing punches. He was so focused on beating the man senseless that he didn't realize there was another man behind him, until just before the guy grabbed him. Sebastian did his best to shift out of the man's grasp, but he had a good hold. Still, Sebastian rolled to the side, taking him off his feet. Turning to grapple with the second man, Sebastian heard Sierra scream, and his head snapped around to look toward the house.

That's when the man pulled out a knife, and shoved it into Sebastian's shoulder. Sebastian gave a yell, but used the adrenaline rush to put all the strength he had into turning to slam his fist into the man's face. He then yanked the knife out of his shoulder, shoving it into his opponent's chest and kicking the man away from him at that same time. He moved to run toward the house, but his first opponent hadn't been completely immobilized and grabbed his leg as he ran by, causing Sebastian to stumble and smash through the back slider. Even so, he jumped to his feet scanning the room.

The front door stood wide open, and he caught sight of red taillights and realized that a third person had obviously gotten into the house and grabbed Sierra and Colby. Using the last of his strength he tried to sprint after the car, but to no avail. He ended up stumbling and falling to the ground, banging his already screaming shoulder.

"Fuck!" he yelled again. He'd just let Kashena down.

Forcing himself to his feet he ran back to the house, pulling out his gun as he entered. Moving through to the back of the house he saw the first assailant on the patio trying to pick up the man Sebastian had knifed.

"Don't fucking move," Sebastian said, his tone all cop at that moment.

The man put his hands up, turning to face Sebastian.

"What the fuck do you mean?" Sebastian asked not for the first time. "Kashena was a Marine you idiot!"

"Not what he told us," the guy said, shaking his head.

"He's a fucking con, you fucking moron!" Sebastian said, punching the man in the face, not for the first time.

"Where the fuck is she!" Sebastian snarled. "Tell me or I swear to fucking God I will kill you right now."

"Downtown, okay, downtown!" the man said, tired of taking punishment from this guy and thinking that Jason wasn't exactly who he'd made himself out to be.

"Give me an address…" Sebastian growled.

"Five twenty-two North A street," the guy said immediately. "Basement."

"Good," Sebastian said, slamming a fist into the man's face knocking him out cold.

He strode out to his Hummer, getting in as he called for backup.

"Jericho, it's me, I know where she's at. Five twenty-two North A Street. I'll be there as fast as I can. No lights, no sirens, and don't let them go in, he'll kill her instantly."

"Got it," Jericho said, nodding.

It was an hour down to the city, he'd have to push it. He just prayed he could make it in time.

"Kashena!" Sierra screamed when she saw her wife lying on the floor with blood all around her.

Kashena stirred, pushing herself up to sitting.

"I'm okay, honey," she said, her voice as soothing as possible.

"Not for long, bitch," Jason said, as he cuffed Sierra and then Colby to a pipe near the door of the room.

He walked over to Kashena; she couldn't get up because of her leg. Lightning fast, Jason got behind her, kneeling and grabbing her by a handful of her hair again. He drew out a knife and held it to her throat. His eyes were on Sierra who was crying.

"Jason no!" Sierra said, her voice tearful. "Please don't!"

Colby stood watching the scene before him, unable to believe his eyes. He yanked at the cuffs that held him, willing to break his hands if he had to get out of them. He had to do something!

"Jason, stop!" he yelled. "Let my mother go, you coward!"

Jason's eyes turned to him then. "You call this bitch your mother?" he said, his tone sneering. "What kind of faggot are you turning into?" he asked.

"As long as I'm not like you," Colby said, his look disgusted.

"I'm a Marine you little pussy," Jason snapped.

"So is my mother and she's a better Marine that you ever were!" Colby yelled.

Kashena knew she needed to do something. She couldn't let Jason near Colby. He'd kill him. Especially with what he was saying. She shifted her weight trying to shove back against Jason, as she did she felt the knife bite into her throat.

"What the fuck do you think you're gonna do?" Jason asked, tightening his hold on her hair painfully.

Kashena's eyes connected with Sierra's, she looked to Colby then, and saw that he was crying now too. She felt tears sting the back s of her eyes as she looked back at Sierra again.

"I love you," she mouthed to Sierra, then closing her eyes, she gathered all of her strength and shoved up and back to put Jason off balance.

She heard Sierra scream as Jason not only didn't go down, but viciously slid the knife across Kashena's throat. She felt the cold of the steel and the burn of the cut and immediately felt her blood pouring out, she knew she'd be dead in minutes. She felt Jason let go of her hair, and she used every ounce of strength she had left to turn and grab him in a bear hug. He struggled to free himself, turning her so he could slam her against the wall to loosen her hold on him. As she sank to the floor she heard Sebastian's voice yell Jason's name and then gunshots. Jason felt on the floor next to her, shot through the head.

Good, he died before me, was Kashena's last thought as everything faded to black.

"Damnit, damnit!" Sebastian yelled, running to Kashena's body, and sliding to his knees. He picked her up seeing the blood pouring from her throat. "Get the fuck in here and call an ambulance now!" he yelled at his backup.

Sebastian felt for a pulse and found the faintest flutter.

"Don't you dare die on me, Marine..." Sebastian growled, sliding his finger down her neck, and feeling for where the blood was flowing from.

He felt her jugular and felt it pulsing as it pumped blood. Pressing his finger against it, he prayed he could do something, anything, to spare her life.

"Don't die on me, Kash... don't die..." he said, unknowingly rocking back and forth as he held his partner in his arms.

The officers who'd followed Sebastian down had uncuffed Colby and Sierra. Sierra ran to where Sebastian held Kashena, her hands shaking as she reached out to touch her wife's face. It felt cold.

"Where's the ambulance?!" Sebastian yelled to no one in particular.

"Coming sir!" someone yelled back.

Sebastian heard the ambulance pulling up outside then.

"Come on, Kash, they're here, you gotta hold on..." Sebastian said.

Sierra was crying, unable to form words at that moment. Colby stood staring at them, trying to understand why this was happening.

The paramedics came running into the room, taking Kashena's lifeless body out of Sebastian's arms. Moving to stand, he helped Sierra up, hugging her to him as the paramedics worked on Kashena.

"I don't have a pulse!" one EMT said.

"Let's go!" the other said.

"We're going with," Sebastian said, grabbing Colby and walking toward the door, Sierra still under one arm.

"Sir, there's too many!"

"Don't care!" Sebastian yelled.

They followed the EMTs out to the ambulance and Sebastian had Sierra and Colby get into the back, he climbed into the passenger side, not willing to argue. The EMTs shrugged and threw on the lights and sirens to get Kashena to the hospital.

It was the longest ten-minute ride of their lives and they could not get Kashena's pulse back. Even so they started an IV and pushed as much fluid into her as they could. The EMT working on her had Sierra put her finger to the jugular vein as Sebastian had, hoping against hope it would help.

Kashena Windwalker-Marshal was officially dead for fifteen minutes. She'd been taken into the emergency room with no pulse. The emergency room doctors worked on her feverishly, trying to repair the damage to the jugular, all the while pumping blood into her body. Suddenly there was a beat on the monitor. Sierra, who was leaning heavily against Sebastian in an almost catatonic state, heard the sound and her head snapped up.

Moving to the side of the gurney that the doctors weren't on, Sierra grabbed Kashena's hand.

"Kashena!" she yelled. "You can do this... come back to me..." she said, her tears flowing once again.

Colby move to join his mother, reaching out to put his hand over Sierra's.

"Mom?" he said. "You can't leave us like this, okay? You gotta come back…"

"Yeah, get your ass back here, Marine!" Sebastian bellowed.

The heart beat continued, slowly at first and then getting stronger.

"That's it…" Sierra whispered next to Kashena's ear. "You can do this… come back to me…"

Sierra was shocked when she felt Kashena's hand squeeze hers slightly. Later, the doctors would tell her there was no way Kashena could have been conscience enough to do such a thing, but Sierra never believed it, not once.

***

Sierra sat in the hospital room where Kashena was recovering. She hadn't regained consciousness yet, but the doctors said that was to be expected with as much trauma as her body had sustained. They'd removed the bullet from her leg and it was healing well.

Sebastian walked in, seeing Kashena lying in the hospital bed. Her eyes were blackened from the blood loss and trauma, and she was very pale, but she was alive and that was all that mattered to him.

"So," he said, moving to sit down next to Sierra. "Do you think you can collect on a life insurance policy if the person was technically dead?" he asked.

Sierra looked back at him like he'd lost his mind. "What are you talking about?"

"Well, Kash took out a two million dollar life insurance policy on herself, knowing she was going to die."

"What?" Sierra asked, completely shocked.

Sebastian pressed his lips together, his look serious now. "She knew she was going to die," he repeated.

"How?" Sierra started to ask, but then understanding dawned in her eyes. "She had a vision…" she said, her voice trailing off as she closed her eyes looking pained.

Sebastian nodded to confirm it, looking a bit stricken himself.

"Why didn't she tell me?" Sierra asked, looking saddened.

He shook his head. "I don't think she saw the point in upsetting you."

"But she told you," Sierra said.

"Yeah, and a lot of times I wished she hadn't."

"That's why you were so pissed at me," Sierra said.

Sebastian nodded. "You were wasting what little time you had left with her."

Sierra grimaced at his words, but knowing that he was right. She looked over at Kashena, reaching over to touch her hand, taking it in her own.

"So you two were going through all of that alone," Sierra said, her voice subdued as her mind worked through events. "That's why she got so mad at Colby when he said he'd protect her with his life…"

"She knew she was going to die anyway, she didn't want to take either of you out with her," Sebastian said.

Sierra closed her eyes, feeling tears stinging the backs of them. Opening them again, she looked at Sebastian.

"Why does she think she has to be so brave all by herself?" she asked him, honestly wanting to know.

Sebastian shrugged. "She's a Marine," he said, his tone wry. "They think they gotta do everything alone."

Sierra looked back at him. "Like Rangers don't," she said, making a face.

Sebastian chuckled at that, she'd definitely picked up Kashena's habits.

It took a few days, but Kashena woke up, lying in a hospital room with an unimaginable amount of flowers, balloons and get well cards.

She tried to say something, but her voice didn't come out.

"Hi there!" Sierra said, moving to stand, looking down at Kashena, her eyes sparkling. "Don't try to talk right now," she told Kashena. "Everything's all swollen, but you'll be okay soon."

Kashena looked up into Sierra, her eyes asking questions her voice couldn't.

"Jason is dead," Sierra said. "Sebastian managed to beat the location of where Jason was holding you, and us, out of a Marine that attacked him."

Kashena nodded sighing in obvious relief.

"Rest, honey," Sierra told her. "You need to get your strength back."

Kashena nodded again, her eyes already half closed.

It was four days before Kashena could speak loud enough to be heard, and even then it was difficult for her. Colby was visiting; Sierra had insisted that he keep up with his school work, so he was going to school and coming to the hospital as often as he could.

Kashena woke, turning over carefully on her side as she did. Colby was sitting in the chair next to the hospital bed doing homework.

"That's... more... like... it..." Kashena said, her words measured and barely above a whisper.

Colby's head snapped up and a bright smile lit his face. "Mom, hi!"

"Hi," Kashena said.

She slowly reached out her hand to him, and he took it, holding it in both of his, and squeezing it gently.

"You really scared me," he told her, his eyes serious. "You died."

"I'm... sorry..." Kashena said, her eyes reflecting the apology.

"He killed you..." Colby said, his eyes sad.

"He... tried..." Kashena responded.

"I love you, Mom," Colby said, tears in his eyes now.

"Love... you..." Kashena responded, squeezing his hand.

"Please don't die ever again," he said then, his grin starting.

"Ever?" Kashena asked, with a raised eyebrow.

"Nope, you have to live forever," he said, grinning.

Kashena rolled her eyes grinning too.

* * *

Julie Powell went on trial for attempted murder of a police officer. She attempted to claim diminished capacity due to childhood trauma. The District Attorney called Deputy Sherriff Raine Mason to testify. He asked Raine about her experiences growing up in the foster system. She explained in detail the number of homes she'd lived in and the experiences she'd had in each.

Sitting in the audience, Natalia realized that Raine had glossed over some of the worst of her experiences. Raine's life in foster care had essentially been much worse than Julie's, culminating in the loss of her best friend due to violence. Natalia testified against Julie, documenting the times she'd grabbed her, screamed at her and been verbally abusive.

Jake, Julie's friend, had contacted Raine, telling her that she would testify against Julie if that would help the case. She also apologized for what she'd done; explaining that she'd never meant to hurt Raine, just to scare her. Raine didn't believe that for a minute, but she accepted the apology and asked Jake to send a letter to the DA, which she had done. The DA read the letter in court. After that, Julie's case looked extremely weak. She accepted a plea deal that put her in prison for life with the possibility of parole after twenty-five years.

With that, it was over. Natalia and Raine were relieved. Natalia had worried herself nearly sick knowing she'd have to face Julie in court. In the end, it was Raine who'd gotten her through it all. She'd found that living with Raine was the easiest thing she'd ever done. They rarely, if ever, fought, and when they did fight, Raine never raised her voice or her hand to her. Raine showed Natalia what a healthy relationship should look like, and that respecting each other and taking what the other person felt and thought into account, should always be the first thing to do in an argument. Natalia was learning a lot from this woman who'd never been in a relationship before. Natalia was convinced that all of the relationships she'd been in up until that point were just marking time until she found Raine. Now she wanted to hold onto her with both hands. She just hoped she'd be able to do that.

***

Four days later Kashena was sent home from the hospital. That night, Sierra was relieved to curl up next to her wife in their bed. She hadn't realized how much she'd missed Kashena's presence in their house until she'd come home that evening.

"Do you need anything?" Sierra asked, looking up at Kashena.

"Nope," Kashena said, smiling, feeling very happy to be home finally.

"Are you tired?" Sierra asked, her look changing slightly.

Kashena tilted her head, one eyebrow going up slightly. "Why?" she asked, her tone suspicious.

Sierra moved to sit up, looking down at Kashena.

"Baz told me about the vision you had," Sierra said, her tone serious.

Kashena closed her eyes slowly, then opened just one, peering up at her wife. "On a scale from one to ten, how much trouble am I in right now?"

Sierra couldn't help but laugh, not only because of the look she was getting from her wife, but for the words she'd just said.

"Let's just say," Sierra said, putting her hand on her wife's stomach, "that you better not ever, and I mean ever Kashena Windwalker-Marshal, keep something like that to yourself again."

Kashena blew her breath out. "I'm honestly hoping I never have a vision that tells me I'm going to die again, but if I do, I promise you'll be the second to know."

"Second?" Sierra repeated sharply.

"The life insurance salesman will still be my first call," Kashena said, smiling beatifically.

"Oh, and that!" Sierra said, narrowing her eyes.

"Uh-oh…" Kashena muttered, knowing she'd backed into more trouble now.

"You know that was completely illegal right?" Sierra said.

"Not really, no," Kashena said, grinning.

"You knew you were going to die!" Sierra exclaimed. "You had prior knowledge!"

"And the paperwork I signed didn't say a damned word about premonitions," Kashena said just as vehemently.

They stared at each other for a long moment, then started to laugh.

"Okay, you got me there," Sierra said, moving to lie down again.

"Ha," Kashena said. "One for the Marine."

"Yeah, yeah," Sierra said, grinning all the same. She grew serious then. "I'm really glad you didn't die."

"Technically I did," Kashena said, her look just as serious.

"Okay, then I'm glad you didn't stay that way."

"Me too," Kashena said, moving to kiss Sierra's lips.

Sierra reached up to touch Kashena's face, her thumb stroking Kashena's cheek.

"I love you," Sierra said against Kashena's lips.

"I love you," Kashena repeated.

"Don't ever leave me again," Sierra said.

"I'll do my best."

Epilogue

"Come on in," Kashena said, to the newest member of her team, Jet Mathews, noting again how light her green eyes were.

Jet walked in, smiling at Kashena, and glancing around at the house, impressed.

"Nice house, boss," Jet said, her light green eyes sparkling.

"Thanks," Kashena said, nodding toward the backyard. "Everyone's back there. Do you need a drink?"

"Always," Jet said, winking at Kashena, taking note of a fairly hot looking Latina in the kitchen. "Hola," she said to the girl, her smile widening.

"That's Natalia," Kashena said. "Nat, this is Jet Mathews, she's on my team."

Natalia turned, looking at Jet and thinking she was an amazing looking woman. Her hair, like her name was jet black and cut in short layers, giving her a bad girl look. Her really light green eyes were framed with black lashes that were long and thick. She had her own light eyed girl though, so she smiled at Jet.

"Bueno conocerte," Natalia said, testing Jet's Spanish, saying it was good to meet her.

"Sin duda, un placer..." Jet replied in perfectly accented Spanish, saying 'definitely a pleasure' with enough insinuation to make Natalia's eyes widen.

"I speak French and German too, in case you're interested," Jet said, winking at her. "Still working on my Arabic though." Her very charming grin followed the last.

Natalia blew her breath out, shaking her hand to indicate heat, as she grinned and turned to walk out of the kitchen. Jet watched her walk, tilting her head to get a better view.

"Careful," Kashena said to Jet as she handed her a beer. "Her girl-friend is on Cat's team…"

"Is she hot too?" Jet asked, grinning.

Kashena laughed out loud at that. She very much liked this young woman; she was smart, talented and definitely a player to the nth power. Leading the way outside to the backyard where the party was in full swing, Kashena let Jet circulate. She walked back over to Sierra, and handed her wife the wine she'd poured for her, leaning in to kiss her softly on the side of the head. Sierra, who was standing talking to Catalina and Jovina, smiled up at Kashena, reaching up to touch her cheek fondly.

Jet wandered over to where she saw Natalia go, seeing the woman that Natalia handed a bottle of water to. Checking Raine out, Jet could see the attraction. Raine was definitely a soft butch, with dark auburn hair that she wore loose, the curls reached to her low back, definitely hot. Jet sighed to herself, she never went for anyone who was attached. You didn't do that to another lesbian, not cool. Walking over to Natalia, Jet smiled, then looked at Raine.

"Hi," she said, grinning and extending her hand to Raine. "Jet Mathews."

"Jet?" Raine repeated.

"Asks the woman named Raine?" Jet replied.

Raine chuckled at that, nodding. "Good point," she said, her light blue eyes amused.

"I'm on Kash's team," Jet said. "I hear you belong to Cat."

"I do," Raine said, nodding her head. "Glad to hear Kash is finally filling some of her spots," Raine said, rubbing her neck. "The overtime was killin' me."

"Well, I'm here to save the day," Jet said, grinning.

"Tengo mi chicha de vuelta," Natalia said, winking at Raine, saying she would get her girl back.

"Hare mi mejor esfuerzo," Jet replied, saying she would do her best, surprising Raine with not only the fact that she spoke Spanish, but also the fact that she did so with a perfect accent.

"Wow," Raine said, impressed.

"She knows French and German too," Natalia said, grinning.

"She also knows Arabic," Skyler said as she walked over.

"Hey!" Jet's face lit up as she saw Skyler.

"Hey yourself!" Skyler said, moving to hug the other woman.

When they parted Jet looked back at Skyler shaking her head in surprise. "Damn! How the hell are ya, Sky?"

"I'm good," Skyler said, turning to gesture to the woman with her. "Jet Mathews, this is my fiancée Devin James."

Jet's intense smile was back then as she checked out the diminutive, but beautiful Devin. "It is my pleasure…" she said, taking Devin's hand, her light green eyes staring directly into Devin's.

"Easy…" Skyler said, grinning even as she did.

Jet's eyes left Devin's for a moment, looking at Skyler. "What?" she asked innocently.

"Oh fuck that!" Skyler said, laughing. "I know you, and I know that routine."

"What routine?" Devin asked, looking between the two.

Skyler and Jet's eyes were locked, both of them grinning. "The one where she disconcerts everyone with that direct eye contact..." Skyler said, her eyes sparkling as Jet started to grin.

Finally Jet broke the stare laughing and shaking her head. "Damnit!" she said lifting her beer to her lips and taking a long swig.

"It is really a pleasure to meet you," Jet told Devin. "Anyone that can catch that one," she said poking a finger in Skyler's direction, "deserves a medal."

"Gee thanks," Skyler said, shaking her head.

"So how do you two know each other?" Devin asked, looking curious.

"We were in the Middle East together," Skyler told Devin.

Jet nodded, her eyes sparkling mischievously.

"Why do I know there's more?" Devin asked, her tone suspicious.

Jet looked at Skyler and shrugging, she walked away.

Devin continued to stare at Skyler, her look expectant. Skyler watched Jet walk away shaking her head, the woman was a troublemaker. She caught Devin's look, and then noticed that both Raine and Natalia were looking at her too.

"Christ!" she said, grinning. "Okay, we were... well, FWBs for a while."

"FWBs?" Raine repeated, not understanding.

"Friends with benefits," Devin explained her eyes on Skyler, her grin still in place. "Interesting…"

"I need another beer," Skyler said, moving toward the kitchen and in the exact opposite direction that Jet had gone in.

Devin watched Skyler go, chuckling to herself.

Jet walked over to the barbecue area, seeing the only man in evidence standing by it, cussing at the coals.

"Does that usually work?" Jet asked conversationally.

Sebastian glanced over his shoulder, taking in the good looking butch standing behind him.

"You're Jet," he said, his green eyes narrowing slightly.

"I know," she responded. "I've been Jet my whole life," she said, with a wink.

Sebastian chuckled, Kashena was right, the girl was quick.

"Kash tells me you spent some time in the Middle East," he said, pushing a coal over with the tongs he held.

"You are?" Jet asked, her tone expectant.

"Sebastian Bach," he said, wiping his hand on his jeans before extending it to her.

"Kash's partner," Jet said, nodding. "Good to meet you, she has a lot of good things to say about you."

"Yeah, secretly she loves me and wants to stop being a lesbian for me," he said, grinning.

"Hope you're not holding your breath on that one," Jet said, grinning as she glanced over to where Kashena and Sierra stood.

Kashena was standing behind Sierra, her arms wrapped around her wife's shoulders, her head bent, whispering in Sierra's ear, while Sierra smiled and nodded.

Sebastian grinned, seeing how happy his partner was, he knew he was seeing relief and it felt good to know that. The Marine who'd been helping Jason had been captured and sentenced to twenty five years to life for being an accomplice to the attempted murder of a police officer. As had the other three men who'd attacked Sebastian and Sierra at the house that night. It was finally over.

Jet glanced at Sebastian, seeing the loyalty and dedication for his partner on his face. She could see that Sebastian was one of those people that was handy to have on your side. She reached up, clapping him on the shoulder, nodding.

"So, Middle East, yes," Jet said, as Sebastian grinned at her.

"Middle East?" Jericho asked, as she and Zoey walked up to the barbeque.

Sebastian nodded toward Jet. "She was in the Middle East."

"With?" Jericho asked, looking at Jet.

"The US Army," Jet said, grinning. "I understand you're from there," she said, extending her hand to Jericho. "I'm Jet Mathews."

"Kashena's new team member," Jericho said, nodding. "She was trying to get you for months."

"I was a bit entangled in some undercover work," Jet said. "But I'm here now."

Jericho nodded. "Good to have you," she said, and then gestured to Zoey. "This is Zoey, my fiancée."

"Lot of that going around," Jet said, grinning as she extended her hand to Zoey, her smile charming. "Good to meet you."

"A lot of what going around?" Jericho asked, raising an eyebrow.

"Engagements," Jet said, touching the ring on Zoey's left ring finger.

"When you meet the right one, you know," Jericho said, leaning over and kissing Zoey's shoulder.

Jet nodded, her eyes taking on a faraway look for a moment, then she smiled at Jericho.

"So you're from Iran, right?" Jet said, making Jericho smile at the fact that she knew how to say Iran correctly.

"I am."

"Farsi?" Jet asked.

"Bale, man Farsi harf mizanam?" Jericho asked in Farsi.

"Bale, ye kam," Jet replied, her accent once again perfect, saying she spoke it a little. "I'm still working on my Arabic too,"

"Impressive…" Jericho said, seeing why Kashena had wanted this girl.

"I was Military Intelligence," Jet said. "It came in handy that I have a good ear for languages."

"I'd say so," Jericho said, nodding again.

Later, Jet was standing near the pool, her eyes staring unseeing at the water; she was in a different time and place in her head.

"Don't jump," came a Northern Irish accented voice from behind her.

Jet glanced over her shoulder, seeing the red-headed butch she'd seen a few times that night.

"Brought you a real beer," Quinn said, handing Jet a Guinness.

Jet looked at the bottle and nodded, lifting it to her lips and taking a long swig.

Quinn nodded, the new butch was okay with her if she could chug a Guinness.

"Quinn Kavanaugh," Quinn said, extending her hand to Jet.

"Jet Mathews," Jet replied, taking Quinn's hand and shaking it. She looked at Quinn's arm. "How are the boys in green doing this year?" she asked, having seen the Northern Ireland football tattoo on Quinn's arm.

"They're doin' alright," Quinn said. "You follow football?"

"Watched it some when I was in Iraq," Jet said. "Rather play than watch."

"Would ya now?" Quinn said, grinning, nodding to her girlfriend as she walked over. "I like this one," she told Xandy.

"Don't mind Quinn," Xandy said, grinning at her girlfriend. "You were in when you drank Guinness without complaint. I'm Xandy,"

"I know," Jet said, her light green eyes sparkling, as she stared into Xandy's lavender-blue eyes. "Like your music. More so now that you're out."

Xandy could see what everyone at the party was talking about with regards to Jet Mathews. The woman did have a way of staring right into you, and it was very disconcerting.

"I…" Xandy stammered, blinking a couple of times. "Thank you," she said.

Quinn looked between her girlfriend and Jet, shaking her head slowly, Jet Mathews was a menace to lesbian society.

"Easy there…" Quinn said, her grin indulgent.

Quinn was quite confident with her place in Xandy's life. Even so, she found it necessary to take Xandy's hand to pull her closer. She caught Jet's quick grin, and knew that she'd been doing it to get to Quinn. Quinn's eyes connected with Jet's, she narrowed her eyes, even as she grinned widely.

"Yer feckin' dangerous," Quinn told Jet. "Gonna get yer ass knifed if yer not careful."

"I'm always careful," Jet replied, her tongue between her teeth, as she widened her eyes.

Quinn laughed out loud at that, shaking her head.

"What's going on over here?" Jovina asked. "Did I hear soccer?"

"Play or watch?" Jet asked, her tone full of innuendo.

"She does both," Cat inserted as she walked up behind Jovina, her eyes on the newcomer, her look inscrutable.

"Says the one that swings both ways," said Quinn with a chuckle.

Now Jet's eyes moved to Catalina. "Both ways?" she asked, her light green eyes curious.

"Don't get too nervous," Cat said, grinning. "She means between butch and femme."

Jet looked quizzical, raising a jet-black eyebrow. "That could be interesting…"

"Not if you want to live through it," Jovina said, her look sweet, even as her words said the opposite.

"Ohhh…" Jet said, her look non-pulsed. "A hot-tempered Latina…" she said, her look on Cat.

"Oh, I don't think I'd dismiss her too easily," Cat said, grinning.

Jovina looked at Cat with narrowed eyes, Cat winked at her, letting her know that she was letting Jet bait her.

Jet caught the exchange and knew that Catalina Roché was quick, she liked her already. Her lips curled in a knowing grin. Cat looked over at Jet, narrowing her eyes slightly, but then nodded, a grin of her own on her lips. Jet was a new and interesting addition to the group, that was for sure.

"Wouldn't it be nice to have a house like this?" Natalia asked Raine, looking around at the pool and the grounds to the house, her tone wistful.

They stood at the far edge of the grounds looking back at the house.

Raine looked around them, then looked down at Natalia. "Doesn't matter to me, as long as I'm with someone I love," she said, smiling down at her.

Natalia reached up, brushing a rich red curl back from Raine's cheek. "I love your hair like this."

"That's the only reason I'm putting up with it," Raine said, smiling.

Natalia bit her lip, smiling up at Raine. "Me haces muy feliz," she said, *You make me so happy.*

"Espero que siempre hago," Raine replied, *I hope I always do.*

Natalia breathed a sigh, she could never get over how amazing it felt to be able to communicate with Raine in her language, and that Raine would always understand her, no matter what. It said so much and it felt so very right.

"Would you come home with me?" Natalia asked, her voice soft.

Raine looked back at her for a long moment. "Honey, we live together."

"I meant to Mexico," Natalia said. "I want you to meet my parents."

Raine looked back at her. "I will go anywhere with you," she answered simply.

Natalia smiled, even as tears sprang to her eyes. She'd wanted to take Julie home to her parents once when their relationship was good. Julie's response had been, "Why would I want to go there? They don't even speak English."

Raine's answer had been, as always, exactly what she'd needed to hear.

"I love you so much…" Natalia said, leaning into kiss Raine's lips.

Raine pulled her close, her hand sliding into Natalia's hair, caressing her neck, and deepening the kiss. Natalia moaned softly against her lips, pressing closer.

"There ya go!" Quinn yelled, whistling.

"That's what I'm talking about!" Cat yelled, clapping her hands.

Everyone started cat calling and clapping, and Natalia and Raine started to laugh, both of them embarrassed, but not willing to break their embrace.

It was a good party.